**D**o zombies scare the not talking the slow stumble around moaning and tripping over their own feet. Those are easy enough to avoid if you keep alert and don't let them swarm you. I'm talking fast zombies. Ones that will run you down, tear you to pieces, and eat you for supper. Ones that keep coming no matter what damage you do to them.

**D**id any such creatures ever exist, except in people's imaginations?

**U**nfortunately, the answer is yes.

**T**his seventh volume of the Harbinger of Doom saga reveals the truth about them. Their origin. And the terrible threat that they pose.

# BOOKS BY GLENN G. THATER

## THE HARBINGER OF DOOM SAGA
GATEWAY TO NIFLEHEIM
THE FALLEN ANGLE
KNIGHT ETERNAL
DWELLERS OF THE DEEP
BLOOD, FIRE, AND THORN
GODS OF THE SWORD
THE SHAMBLING DEAD
MASTER OF THE DEAD
SHADOW OF DOOM
WIZARD'S TOLL
VOLUME 11+ (forthcoming)

### HARBINGER OF DOOM
(Combines *Gateway to Nifleheim* and *The Fallen Angle* into a single volume)

### THE HERO AND THE FIEND
(A novelette set in the Harbinger of Doom universe)

### THE GATEWAY
(A novella length version of *Gateway to Nifleheim*)

### THE DEMON KING OF BERGHER
(A short story set in the Harbinger of Doom universe)

To be notified about my new book releases and any special offers or discounts regarding my books, please join my mailing list here: http://eepurl.com/vwubH

# GLENN G. THATER

# THE
# SHAMBLING
# DEAD

*A TALE FROM THE
HARBINGER OF DOOM SAGA*

This book is a work of fiction. Names, characters, places, and incidents are either the product of the author's imagination or are used fictitiously. Any resemblance to actual persons, living or dead, events, or locales is entirely coincidental.

THE SHAMBLING DEAD © 2014 by Glenn G. Thater

All rights reserved.

ISBN-13: 978-0692616512
ISBN-10: 0692616519

Visit Glenn G. Thater's website at
http://www.glenngthater.com

January 2016 Worldwide Print Edition
Published by Lomion Press

# FOREWORD

The undead. Creatures alive (or at least, animated), yet dead by any common or medical standards, fill popular culture. Reading about them and watching their rampages on TV and in movies excites us, frightens us, and captures our imaginations in ways few other things do, resulting in the steadfast popularity of George A. Romero's zombie movies, Robert Kirkman's, *The Walking Dead*, Stefanie Meyer's and Ann Rice's vampire books, amongst many others. But where did the legends of such creatures originate? Are they merely products of the modern imagination or do their origins reach back into the distant past, to ancient times? Are they pure fiction? Are they myth? Or allegory? Or are they based on real people, creatures, and historical events?

Ask around and some folks that don't get out much will tell you that George A. Romero invented zombies with his film, *Night of the Living Dead* (1968). Cinephiles will cite Victor Halperin's, *White Zombie* (1932) as the shambling dead's origin. Others will speak of Haitian folklore or remark that Mary Shelley's *Frankenstein* (1818) tells us the first true zombie tale. As for vampires, everyone knows it was Bram Stoker's *Dracula* (1897) that started the vampire craze, and some know that Stoker didn't invent vampires, but rather drew on 18th century folk legends from southeastern Europe. Some few point to the 15th century historical figure, Vlad Tepes, better known as Vlad the Impaler, as the origin of those folk tales.

All of that, as Ob would put it, is hogwash and horsefeathers. The notion of the undead, in general, and that of zombies and vampires in particular, predate all of those modern sources not by hundreds, but by thousands of years.

Case in point, the *Holy Bible*. The Old Testament, Book of Ezekiel, 37:1-14 (sixth century BC) tells the story of the plain of dry bones, wherein creatures resembling the modern notion of zombies rise up from the ground. Ezekiel states that he heard, "*a rattling as the bones came together, bone joining bone. I saw the sinews and the flesh come upon them, and the skin cover them, but there was no spirit in them...they came alive and stood upright, a vast army.*"

*The Epic of Gilgamesh* (1900 BC). You probably read it (or were supposed to read it) in high school, but I doubt you remember the passage wherein the goddess Ishtar declares, "*I will smash the door posts* (of the nether world), *and leave the doors flat down, and will let the dead go up to eat the living!*" Sounds like zombies to me.

Those sources and a few others represent the earliest written references to the undead known prior to about the year 2002 AD. In that year, everything changed. Since that time, several new sources, including The Grenoble Tablets and the scrolls of Corsi and Burdur have been discovered, and previously discovered works, such as the Ashmolean Vellum, the various Scrolls of Cumbria, and the Olmec and Kish tablets, have finally been comprehensively translated. The body of work these sources comprise has been dubbed, Thetian literature — a nod of respect to Theta (aka Thetan), the central character of the works.

What do these stories tell us about the undead?

A lot.

But not just harrowing tales of zombies feasting on the living, and powerful vampires lusting for blood. They tell us about the actual origin of the undead. How and why they came about: what created them! And how the great hero (or is he?), Theta, dealt with them.

Most spectacularly, these tales are presented (by their primal sources) as historical accounts, not stories for entertainment. According to the sources, these events really happened. To the original writers and their intended readers/listeners, the undead were real.

I've studied the translations, and I warn you, some portions of the stories are shocking — so much so, that I thought long and hard before deciding to adapt them to modern prose. In the pages of volumes 7 and 8 of the Harbinger of Doom Saga, I will reveal to you the true origins of the zombie, the vampire, and the wendigo. If you're faint of heart, or just not ready to know the truth, close this book now, and move on to something less haunting, something that won't keep you up at night, fearing every bump, noise, and knock.

Knowing that these things were, at one time, real creatures, and perhaps, given the right circumstances, could still be real, could still be

among us today, should you be afraid?
   Yes, you should be.
   I am.

Glenn G. Thater
New York, USA
2014

# AUTHOR'S NOTE

The source material for the Harbinger of Doom (HOD) saga contains two stand-alone but related stories about the origin of zombies and vampires. That in itself is more than reason enough to bring them to print. But more importantly, for fans of the HOD books, both stories contain plot elements and characters that are central to the main HOD storyline, and inexorably related to Theta's exploits.

One story, untitled in the source documents, but called, *The Bloodlust*, by scholars, takes place some four hundred years prior to the events chronicled in *Gateway to Nifleheim*. The other story, entitled, *Master of the Dead*, takes place twenty-five years prior to *Gateway to Nifleheim*.

My original plan was to present *The Bloodlust* as Volume 7 of the HOD Saga, and *Master of the Dead* as Volume 8. But as I began transforming the latest translations of these tales into modern prose, I realized that because of the interrelationships between the stories, they needed to be weaved together to achieve maximum dramatic effect. Therefore, within Volumes 7 and 8, these two stories unfold in parallel, switching back and forth between them, one to three chapters at a time. I decided not to use "bloodlust" as a title, and instead named Volume 7, *The Shambling Dead*, and Volume 8, *Master of the Dead*. I've also weaved in a few chapters that connect us back to, and progress, the main storyline, from where we left off at the end of Volume 6.

In these pages, you'll visit with Theta, of course (though, I'll admit, not nearly as much as in previous Volumes), but also Sir Gabriel, Ob, Aradon Eotrus, Par Talbon, and many other familiar characters to fans of the Saga. And you'll meet for the first time, the infamous Master of the Dead.

After reading these volumes, I hope that you'll agree that presenting the stories in this manner, at this point in the HOD Saga, was a good choice, and that you enjoy reading them as much as I enjoyed writing them.

# 1

# THE AZURE SEA, ISLE OF EVERMERE, EVERMERE BAY

*Year 1,267, Fourth Age of Midgaard*
*(Year 853 by Lomerian Reckoning)*
*37th Year of King Tenzivel's Rule*

**O**b, that dour old gnome of bulbous nose and bad attitude, couldn't believe it had come to this. Stranded in a stinking longboat with a squad of battered men, no help in sight, and surrounded by blood-sucking cannibals with superhuman powers; thousands of them.

Thousands!

Who ever heard of such a thing? People with powers like that? Strength of men twice their size and more? Take an arrow to the chest as if it was nothing but a bug bite? And wanting to drink people's blood like it was good summer wine? And eat people's flesh?

Eat them!

For Odin's sake, they cook people up in the stew.

Dead gods, it's madness. Stinking crazy no good inbred cannibals is what they are. And they smell too; them buggers don't bathe.

More like a dark faerie story than reality, it was. Like some old tale out of the Age of Myth and

Legend. Such things didn't happen in the modern world, if ever they happened at all. It all made no sense. Not to Ob. Nothing made sense to him for a long time. Not since Mister Fancy Pants, Angle Theta, showed up, that stinking foreign bastard. Since then, the whole world got turned on its head. It went mad, the world did. Ob figured, maybe he'd gone mad along with it.

*The Black Falcon* was gone, shattered and sunk to the bottom of the bay by a sea monster straight from some children's tale. And that same monster took Claradon Eotrus too, pulled him down to the bottom, the poor boy; killed him dead, all the knights of Dor Eotrus and their allies with him. Good men were they, one and all: Kelbor, Trelman, the Bull, young Paldor, Seran Harringgold, and all the rest. They were Ob's friends, that bunch of stinking tin cans. Along with Sir Gabriel, he'd trained up most of them from when they was but pups. Good men. From good families. All gone.

They were important to him, those men. Heck, he didn't have many friends left. Not on Midgaard anyways. The rest were all dead. All called up Valhalla way. Or pulled down to Helheim. Or wherever else men went when they got dead.

Ob figured that after all that Claradon had been through, he shouldn't have died like that — without even having a chance to defend himself. To have survived that terrible chest wound from that stinking Pict mercenary, and get healed up where most any other man would have died outright, and then to be killed like that, by a thing — a sea beast the size of a small mountain.

It wasn't fair. It wasn't right. There was no justice to it. But that was the way of life. Especially for a soldier. Things didn't work out fair. Except when you got lucky.

Hopefully, the Valkyries took Claradon, carried him on up Valhalla way, and the other knights with him too. As far as Ob was concerned, they'd all earned their places in Odin's hall for past deeds, good and proper.

Maybe Claradon and them others sat at the all-father's table even now, drinking and feasting, boasting and bragging about their exploits. Maybe Claradon sat shoulder to shoulder with his parents, Aradon and Eleanor — dear Eleanor. How she loved Claradon. How proud of him she was. And his grandpap, old Lord Nardon, will be there with them, watching over his brood. Now at least, they're together again. Or should be if there's any justice in the afterlife. Par Talbon will be beside them. Stern too. And stinking Brother Donnelin. In some ways, he missed Donnelin most of all.

Maybe, at that very moment, they gazed down from Asgard on their sorry friends as they met their fate in this terrible battle, the gods watching along with them: Odin, Thor, Heimdall, Tyr, and the rest. Not every day was there a battle like this fight against the Evermerian bloodsuckers. Not every day did such great warriors fall.

Maybe Claradon, or one of the others, would think kindly enough of old Ob to put in a good word for him with the gods. And if they did, maybe the Valkyries would keep their eyes peeled for him, so that when he fell in battle they'd notice him straightaway, scoop him up on one of them winged horses of theirs, and carry him on up Odin's way too. Or so Ob hoped.

All that remained of the ill-fated Eotrus expedition were those sorry bastards crammed into the longboat with Ob, a few of them already on death's door. But what a bunch. A wrecking crew like no other that Ob had known; every man amongst them worthy of leading a troop of Odin's best in Valhalla, or so Ob figured.

They'd killed more of them bloodsuckers than they could count — mostly Par Tanch's doing. Good old Magic Boy had blasted them with a firestorm that'd be the envy of the greatest firedrakes of legend. How he managed it, Ob couldn't imagine. And Theta had pulled out every trick in the book to hold the cannibals back. And when he got done with the book, he came up with more tricks — stratagems that Ob had never seen before, never even heard of. But it wasn't enough. There were just too many of them, the bloodsuckers. They just kept coming.

Dolan Silk, Theta's simpleton manservant (who Ob suspected wasn't nearly as simple as he seemed), had made a good account of himself. Even as bruised and broken as he was, his arrows knocked a dozen Evermerian boats out of action.

A full dozen!

And all by his lonesome. From recent days, Ob knew that Dolan was a crack shot; an expert. But he'd never seen nor heard tell of any shooting like Dolan had done on that longboat. If Ob hadn't seen it himself, he would never have believed it. He figured that that boy was the best archer in all Midgaard, and not just now, but ever. Which was funny, because from just looking at him, you wouldn't think Dolan had any skills at all. Nothing special at least.

Dolan even put an arrow through the Duchess's face, that stinking witch. But that didn't end her or the attack. On they came, the bloodsuckers did. Intent on killing them all — except for Theta and Tanch, for the stinking Duchess ordered their capture. She had "*plans for them*," whatever that meant.

Par Tanch was down and out, unconscious from the effects of his own magic. There was nothing to stop the bloodsuckers from taking him, save the swords of his fellows about him.

But Theta was battle ready. He would kill ten men's share at least. In the end though, that wouldn't matter. No man could stand against the army that came at them. Force of numbers would eventually take him down.

Them two, Theta and Tanch, might get captured like the Duchess ordered. And with that came some hope for them, however slim. But for the rest of them, it was the end, for the Duchess ordered her people to kill them, dead.

Ob figured that Old Death had finally caught up to him. Was bound to happen sometime; the reaper had chased him for more than three hundred years with little to show for it. He had denied Old Death almost everything what was his due. Despite all the fighting he had done, Ob still had both eyes, both ears, all twelve fingers, and most of his teeth; he even had his hair, some of it anyways.

But Ob didn't think the skein of his life was on

its last thread yet. There was too much important stuff what still needed doing — like stopping Korrgonn, for one. All of Midgaard depended on that.

If not Ob and his crew, who'd stop the Nifleheim lord? Who would block his evil plans to open up another gateway to Nifleheim and bring forth Azathoth to rule over Midgaard once again? Who else was even trying?

No one.

It all depended on them. Everything did.

Or did it?

Ob wondered whether thinking that made him a fool; to think that he was too important to die. Took a lot of pride to think that — that his time hadn't come yet, despite the sorry circumstances; that maybe it would never come. Or should never come. Lots of fools thought such things. Believed them with every ounce of strength and will in their minds and bodies. Did that stop Old Death from walking off with their souls?

Nope. It did not.

Ob figured that if he had to die, at least he was amongst good company. The toughest bunch of killers he could imagine sat their butts alongside him, Theta, and Dolan, in that longboat. Stinking Little Tug — seven feet tall, and near as wide. He'd ripped a bunch of them bloodsuckers apart with his bare hands. All their strength, speed, and resilience were little help against him and his huge hammer, Old Fogey.

Artol, just as tall, and even meaner, had killed his share of the cannibals, and then some; no tougher man or better warrior was there in all

Midgaard.

Captain Dylan Slaayde of *The Black Falcon* had done his part too, the old sea dog. He might look like a rotund dandy, but the man was tough. And darned hard to kill.

Captain Graybeard, the grizzled seaman that they'd rescued from the bloodsuckers' clutches had shown his mettle too; him and the last couple of survivors from his schooner. Ob didn't know those other sailors' names; not that it mattered, since they'd all be dead soon.

And last was Glimador Malvegil (son of Torbin) — Claradon's cousin and boyhood pal, a fine, fearless knight and secret wizard, trained up by his mother. His father would be proud; his mother too — but best not to think about her.

A few more moments and the bloodsuckers would board the longboat, or else swamp it. On solid ground, Ob and the men would fight back to back, and make them scum suckers bleed for every inch. But on the longboat, there was no firm footing, no room to maneuver. You couldn't fight your best, not nearly. But that was the way of war, and Ob knew that all too well. Battles didn't happen only when you were at your best: healthy, strong, well-fed and rested, and on good ground. In fact, most times, battles happened when you were at your worst: wounded, tired, sick, and such. That was a soldier's lot in life. And most of the men with Ob were soldiers, born and bred. Not Bertha, the poor lass, her throat bit open by one of them things, maybe dead already. And Par Tanch, soon to follow on her heels. Tanch's own magic, had done him in. Burned him from the inside. Fried his brain, the poor bastard. And to think, Ob had made fun of him for years for being a useless, whiny sot. If not for him, they'd all already be dead.

Ob had his axe in one hand, his dagger in the other. He'd give them what for when they came at him. He'd go out fighting; that's the gnome way, you know.

A warrior's death.

That's all Ob had ever wanted. He wasn't ready for it, but he wasn't afraid of it either.

Ob sat at the rear of the boat, manning the tiller. Why he got that duty when there were seamen aboard, he didn't know. But it always seemed to be his spot on the longboat, and he was good at it, so he made no complaint.

Ob looked down the line of men. Theta at the far side. For the first time ever, the man looked weary, beaten. Ob never thought he'd see him like that. But as the devils drew closer, Theta stood tall, his expression defiant.

All the men on the longboat stood poised to repel borders. As Ob hunched there, staring down that line of soldiers, staring at Theta at the far end, his mind drifted to another day, another time when he sat in a longboat filled of men just like that. Another wrecking crew they were.

# 2
# THE DEAD FENS

*Year 1242, Fourth Age
Twelfth Year of King Tenzivel's Rule*

Ob sensed that something was about to happen. Something bad.

He could feel it in his bones. He could almost smell it. And he knew that the big knight sensed it too. And yet old Mister High-and-Mighty Hero just stood there, oblivious, as if there weren't nothing in all Midgaard what could harm him.

And maybe there wasn't.

The bastard was near as tough as Odin himself, or so Ob figured.

You'd think that he'd have sense enough not to stand at the longboat's bow while they slogged through the Dead Fens — what with the muck that kept hanging them up, the countless deadfalls and brambles that needed dodging, and the mist as thick as Brother Donnelin's cabbage soup (and with a stink even worse) that made seeing nigh impossible.

When you rowed through that swamp, one moment you could be standing tall, the next you'd be dumped into the drink, if you were lucky, or onto some spikey wood or sharp stones if things went against you.

But there, perched at the bow, was the great man, looking out into the mist, putrid swamp stuff and low visibility be damned. Affected by none of it was old Mister Know-it-All.

Mister Confidence.

Mister Invulnerable.

Sometimes, just looking at him sent a chill up Ob's spine.

Ob was never afraid of anyone. Not one other man he'd met in over three hundred years of soldiering, adventuring, and exploring.

But he was afraid of that man, if a mortal man he even was. More afraid of him than he was of Old Death himself.

And yet, as time passed, and they'd fended off Old Death together time and again, Ob had come to love Mister Bigshot as if he were his own brother — not that he'd ever admit it, and he had some doubts that the feeling was mutual.

Swamp gas hung all about the outskirts of the Dead Fens. It percolated up from the mud, bubbling, wheezing, and popping. Here and there, little bursts of flame shot up out of the muck. They'd burn your tail clean off if you were in the wrong spot at the wrong time. But just as quick, the flames got gone whence they came.

Sometimes, a little spot on the muck suddenly ignited and burned like a candle for who knows how long before it sputtered out. How and why such things went on in the Fens, none could say for certain. Some thought it due to powerful magics gone awry back in olden days. They figured some remnant of that power lingered about, mucking up the place.

Ob figured it was natural. Chemicals or some such in the ground, mixing together in just the right amounts: add some water, air, and time, and sit back and watch the show. Alchemists played with such stuff all the time. Some were masters of it. You could make fireworks that sparked and shot way up in the air, with the right powders and such, if you knew what you were doing. Ob had seen it. More than once. Nothing unnatural about it. Not everything what folks don't understand is magic.

In fact, not much of anything is, or so Ob figured.

Some fools just wallowed in their ignorance. They wore it on their sleeves and let it dribble from their mouths most times they opened them. Let the stupids keep their superstitions if they wanted to. Ob would have none of it. Especially not when he was tired and cold. And he was darned tired. He was getting too old for these kinds of missions.

Heck, he'd been too old for a long time.

They'd rowed and levered their way with long poles for hours into the Fens after leaving the Grand Hudsar River, though the vapors were a barrier that repeatedly threatened to turn them back and caused them to waste much time backtracking and diverting around the worst of it.

A darned good barrier it was. And its message was clear:

*Keep out of the Fens. Go back. This be no place for you.*

And it worked. Always had. It kept out the lookeyloos, the wanderers, the explorers, and the would-be adventurers — even the ones what knew what they were doing, which weren't many as far as Ob was concerned.

But it didn't keep out the stupids. Nothing ever did that. Some of them wandered in once in a while, all smiles and picnic baskets, ripe for adventure and discovery. They rarely wandered out again, and even then, only if they'd stuck to the very outskirts. One way or another, the Fens took them if they dared venture into the deeps (which was exactly where Ob and company were headed, of course).

And yet, more of them always came; the stupids. And so, the vapors preserved the mystery of the Dead Fens despite its proximity to civilization — situated as it was, just downriver from Dor Malvegil, on the eastern bank of the Hudsar. Looming there like a big infected boil, just waiting to sneak up on you all unexpected like and snatch your life away.

Ob and the others tried to keep out the bog's stench and whatever it was in those vapors what made a man retch. Wet rags dipped in a peppermint oil mixture over their mouths and noses. Nonetheless, the fumes proved skillful at clogging up their throats, making them gasp and cough up yellow-colored phlegm, except for some what came out puke green and thick enough to choke a man dead. Ob had sent his share of it over the longboat's side along the way, just as the others had, though for some reason or other, the stench bothered him less than it did the others. Probably because he was hardier than them, or so Ob figured.

Or maybe his nose just didn't work so good anymore. Maybe it was tired and worn out like the rest of him.

Ob manned the longboat's tiller and tried to avoid running them aground as he watched for any sign or signal from Mister High-and-Mighty (as best he could watch through the mist), though he could hardly see anything past the wrecking crew that filled the boat.

Eotrus men and Malvegils they were.

One dozen even.

Handpicked by Malvegil's witch wife — a temptress, that one was: curves like a goddess; pretty as a rose, thorns and all; tough as a Valkyrie; and more than she seemed. Best not to even look at her, Ob figured, lest a man risk losing his heart and maybe worse. Best not to even think about her.

She'd chosen wisely, for to a man, they were the toughest bunch that Ob had ever known — not a dandy, pretty boy, rookie, or tourney knight amongst them. Only true warriors were they, with a few stinking magic boys (as Ob called wizards, irrespective of age or skill) mixed in for good measure.

Ob figured that old Mister Hero sensed the danger too. Not much got past that fellow. He'd been acting all squirrelly for the previous hour and kept fingering his ankh thingy — that weird religious thingamabob what he wore about his neck. The ankh was a relic left over from ancient days; maybe even from as far back as the Age of Heroes. How it hadn't fallen apart or crumbled to dust, Ob couldn't figure. The big man relied on it for all sorts of stuff. Consulted it time and again. More so even than he consulted Ob. As if the thing knew anything; the stinking piece of wood or whatever it was. It was downright insulting, relying on such a thing over a good gnome's counsel. Superstitious drivel.

From his perch at the bow, the tall, enigmatic soldier of ancient eyes and lordly looks whispered a single word.

"Hold."

Ob didn't hear him, superior gnome hearing notwithstanding, owing to the innumerable insects and other small creatures whose incessant chirping, chattering, and gibbering clogged his ears and drowned out most every other sound in the Fens. But the knight's hand signals were clear enough.

*Go silent.*
*Go still.*
*Stay the oars.*

So signaled Sir Gabriel Garn — longtime ally of the Eotrus, and arguably, the most renowned knight in all the Kingdom of Lomion.

# 3

# THE DEAD FENS

*Year 1242, Fourth Age
Twelfth Year of King Tenzivel's Rule*

Sir Gabriel looked from side to side as he stood there at the longboat's prow dressed in bluish gray and black, his features carved of solid granite, his black ponytail hanging halfway down his back.

He could not have seen much through the foggy miasma of the Dead Fens. Generous patches of shallow but open water, interspersed between a maze of floating muck and mounds of mud and vegetation, stretched out around the longboat in all directions.

Gabriel's left hand slowly moved to his sword's hilt; his right hand continued to command silence.

After a moment, a loud croaking noise, not of a frog or toad but of something much larger, much more dangerous, erupted from off to port, away in the mist. Instantly, the Fen went silent.

Not an insect, not a bird was heard.

Nothing.

It was as if all life in the bog froze in panic and held its breath, hoping to escape the notice of what was coming.

Gabriel carefully slid his sword from its sheath, still staring into the mist. The slight hum that the blade made as it slid out seemed thunderous in the silence.

The men behind Gabriel gazed warily about, hands on their weapons, but the haze limited their sight, the mist wafting and swirling about them.

No one dared speak; it was tough enough to muster the courage to breathe.

Gabriel turned his head toward the men, his eyes wide. "Back us out," he hissed. "Be quick!"

A moment later, a gurgling, choking noise exploded from off starboard. Then something large splashed the water on one side of the boat. A similar splash followed it from the other side, though whatever it was, was still out of sight.

More splashing came from up ahead.

They were moving closer, whoever or whatever they were, and coming at the longboat from three sides at least: a coordinated assault. They must have heard the longboat coming.

Ripples in the water lapped against the boat.

The men followed Gabriel's command. Even the two great lords that were amongst them.

They put down their weapons and pulled on the oars.

They pulled hard.

One stroke and then another. Anxious to get away. They weren't afraid of whatever was out there.

Not those men.

But not one amongst them wanted any part of a battle while sitting in a longboat in the middle of a bog. There was no way to maneuver. No sure footing in the boat. And less so in the water. They needed to get out of there. To get themselves to dry land before engaging the enemy; whoever the enemy was.

"Too late," said Gabriel. He sprang up, sword humming through the chill air faster than the eye could follow. He swung his blade through the mist that swirled about the prow. It sliced into something hidden by the vapors, though whatever it was, made no sound as it took the blow.

Gabriel slashed again. And then a third time, each a powerful stroke. Ob never saw what it was, the stinking mist so thick, but Gabriel's sword came back covered in gore.

As one, the men scrambled for their weapons. Ob's eyes widened and the hair on the back of his head stood up when he saw one humanlike hand and then another, pale, bloated, and wicked-nailed, grasp the gunwale behind Par Rorbit (House Wizard for the Malvegils). Before Ob could cry out a warning, a head sprang up from the water — gray and hairless, its mottled flesh hanging loose. Its visage resembling, as much as anything, a month old human corpse fished out of the sea. The creature reached for Rorbit. Its claws, ragged and grimy. It opened its maw. From it, issued a thunderous croaking — a wild, eerie sound; too loud, too alien, to come from the throat of any man.

Despite vast experience and his usual poise, Rorbit yelped, jerked to the side, and fumbled for his dagger.

Beside him, Torbin Malvegil – brawny young lord of black mane and toothy grin, pulled a dagger, fire in his eyes.

The creature tried to heave itself into the boat. But Malvegil was the quicker. He slammed his dagger into one of the creature's milky eyes.

The blade sank to its hilt.

No blood spurted from the terrible wound. No cry of pain sprang from the thing's lips. Malvegil looked stunned by its lack of reaction.

The thing began to slide back into the water.

Ob figured it was dead, or else, it had no fight left in it. Who would, after a dagger to the eye?

But then its hand shot out. It grabbed Rorbit's leg. Its filthy claws dug into his calf: ripped through his pant, and sliced ragged furrows into his flesh.

Rorbit howled in pain.

As the creature slid back into the water, it dragged Rorbit to the gunwale. What strength it had, for the wizard was a large man, and fought the thing for every inch. Rorbit grabbed for handholds and kicked the creature over and again.

Sir Gabriel's voice cut through the mist. "Keep rowing," he shouted. Ob couldn't say whether the men complied; all his attention focused on the melee with the creature.

Rorbit leaned forward. He clamped one hand to the creature's forehead and gripped one of the oarsmen's benches to steady himself with the other. He mouthed ancient words of the *Magus Mysterious*, that olden tongue that wizards used to tap the Grand Weave of Magic from which they derived their powers.

Rorbit's hand glowed. Just for a moment. That's all it took.

The creature's head exploded. Bits of bone and brain flew in all directions, pelting the water and the men in the boat.

The creature's remains slid limply over the gunwale into the murky water, this time, never to rise again.

As Rorbit leaned over the gunwale barking curses, two pairs of mangled hands, bones peeking through their flesh, reached up out of the water. They grabbed him. By both his arms.

Malvegil for him. That time, he wasn't quick enough.

Rorbit went over the side with a yowl. He plunged face first into the water and disappeared beneath its inky surface.

A moment later, there was a great thrashing and commotion in the water. The creatures had set upon the wizard. How many, Ob couldn't say, but there were surely more than just the two that had pulled him in.

The men in the longboat dropped their oars. They'd not abandon one of their own. Several were about to go over the side to aid Rorbit when a subsurface flash of light erupted from where he went under, followed by a terrific bang that echoed across the Fens.

A water plume shot up from that spot. Rorbit was giving them what for: magic and such. Then more flashes and subsurface explosions — one after another; a half dozen at least, all within the space of a few moments.

The water roiled; the boat rocked, spun, and threatened to capsize. Cold, putrid spray drenched the men. And a strange, burning scent hovered in the air.

And then the boat crashed.

It slammed into something. Something where nothing should have been.

Something that stopped it dead.

Gabriel fell onto the men behind him. Everyone else standing also fell; some overboard. Those who were seated, slid off their benches or flopped over. Ob went flying over the gunwale, seat-first into the water.

At once, a dozen creatures of nightmare popped up, heads, shoulders, and torsos, out of the murky water all around the boat, just close enough for the men to see them despite the mist. Horrid, monstrous things were they, like the one that attacked Rorbit. Dark shadows behind them promised more of their brethren loomed farther out, still hidden by the murk. All of them croaked and barked — painful sounds, both in volume and pitch.

They hurled themselves at the longboat.

They tried to pull themselves aboard.

They grabbed for the men; their eyes, maniacal; their stench, unbearable; their hunger, unspeakable and insatiable.

# 4

# DOR MALVEGIL
# LORD MALVEGIL'S
# PRIVATE QUARTERS

*Year 1242, Fourth Age
Twelfth Year of King Tenzivel's Rule*

Torbin Malvegil awoke with a start. "What is it? What's happened?" he said sharply as he scrambled out of the bed, blinking, his vision fuzzy from sleep. His hand found his sword, which rested in its usual spot next to the bed. His consort, Lady Landolyn, was sitting up in bed, breathing heavily. Their bedchamber's door was closed and barred, the window too. Nothing seemed out of place. No strange odors hung in the air. No intruder lurked at the foot of the bed.

"A vision," she said.

Torbin sighed. "Another? What is it this time?" he said as he sat back down on the bed and rubbed the sleep from his eyes. No light showed through the large windows. It was not yet dawn.

"You will receive ill news today," said Landolyn. "With that news comes a danger; a grave danger, though of its nature, I cannot yet say."

"Could it be naught but a dream?" said Malvegil.

This time, she sighed. "Again you disbelieve me?" she said, her voice sharp. "You question me?

It's so frustrating."

"Of course, I question," said Malvegil. "What kind of leader would I be if I didn't question? If I accepted everything blindly?"

"You're not my leader; you're my husband."

"I am both, make no mistake, woman," said Malvegil. "And I make no apologies for questions, but I don't disbelieve you."

"You think there's nothing between my ears but fluff and feathers, like the foolish women at court."

"You know that's not true," said Torbin.

"You don't respect me, or my abilities."

"I do," he said, "but people dream. People have nightmares. Not everything is a vision or a prophecy sent down from who knows where."

Landolyn narrowed her eyes. "You think that I don't know the difference? My powers did not appear from nowhere just last night, you know. I've had them all my life, my mother before me, her mother before her, and on and on, back unto olden days. I know well the difference between a dream and a vision. What I have told you will come to pass. You need not believe me, for the truth will soon be evident. But you must believe me, for my gifts can be a great boon to you, if used properly. Do not scoff at or squander what I offer. You have made little use of my skills since we've been together."

"I know your powers," said Malvegil. "Both the obvious and the esoteric. And I value them all."

"Do you?" she said, smiling as he stared at her, her nightdress sheer and low cut. "Or are my curves and my pretty face all that you truly value?

That's what the nobles say, isn't it? The high-and-mighty gossiping feather-headed know-it-alls of Lomion City. Why else would the great lord of the Malvegils consort with a woman of the" (elven) "blood? A witch woman, no less? Isn't that what they say? That I've bewitched you with my wiles or my magic?"

"I care naught for what tumbles from the mouths of fools," said Malvegil.

She moved to a kneeling position on the bed, the better for him to see her. "Then perhaps you should," she said. "For I could bewitch you. I could do it easily," she said as she slowly moved her hands from her thighs up to her breasts. "I can bewitch any man that I like — most without using any hint of magic."

"But with magic, I could make them my slaves. I could have anything that I want. Anything. I could rule." She paused a moment and let that statement sink in.

Torbin narrowed his eyes, but held his tongue, waiting for her to continue.

"But that is not my way," she said. "And I have never bewitched you, husband. Not with magic, at least," she said, a coy smile appearing on her face, her voice growing softer.

"And you must never try," he said with a serious tone, an edge to his voice.

"Many of your Volsung women are pretty, are they not?"

"I suppose. What of it?"

"But not so pretty as me? Not many, anyway."

"I have never seen any other as beautiful as you," said Malvegil.

"And these," she said, cupping her hands against her breasts. "They don't have these. Not like mine. Not a third as big, maybe not even a quarter; not even the fat ones. Or this," she said, touching her hips. "Volsung girls are not half as wide or as round here as I am."

"This be true," he said, staring at her hips. "Not nearly half."

"Well I am more than these things," she said. "Much more. Don't be blinded by them and fail to see me."

"I can see little else."

"Aargh, you are a fool. A pompous fool like all Volsungs. Like all men."

He reached out and grabbed her, firmly, but not harshly. He pulled her close. He kissed her on the lips. She resisted for a moment, but only for a moment. "Tell me of your vision," he said. "Tell me all; tell me clear; tell me true. Leave nothing out. And when you are done, then you may bewitch me — just a bit, but not with magic."

She smiled. "Yes, my lord."

# 5

# THE DEAD FENS

*Year 1242, Fourth Age
Twelfth Year of King Tenzivel's Rule*

**O**b, momentarily stunned from the boat's crash and the frigid water he plunged into, quickly found his footing. The water was shallow, but Ob's three-foot-six height did him little service, the water up to his nose.

A dark shape rose up before him. Like a man it was, but not a man.

A thing.

A thing out of a nightmare.

It towered over Ob — near as tall as Artol, but twice as thick. The flesh of its face and body was torn and mangled; its eyes, milky white; its skin, sallow. Worse still, it was rotted to the core. Its aspect and putrid stench akin to a corpse a week or more old and water-bloated, dripping of water, muck, and slime.

But it wasn't a corpse. It wasn't dead. It couldn't be, for it moved. And by the look of it, it hungered.

Hungered for Ob's flesh.

But no natural creature could it be. Not with that rot, that stench. Ob had never seen its like. Never heard of anything like it. A demon called up from Helheim, it must have been. Or a devil from the depths of Nifleheim. But then Ob caught himself.

He'd not let superstition take over. That was the gateway to fear, and fear led to hesitation or worse.

In battle, that got you killed.

The creature tried to slash Ob with claw-like hands, even as it bared its teeth.

Ob didn't hesitate; he didn't freeze. He dodged the claws with dexterity that belied his age. He pulled his sword as he had done untold thousands of times before. He thrust it forward, up out of the water.

His aim was true. His blade sank deep — into where the thing's heart should be. Overbalanced, Ob went down on his rump. Right to the muddy bottom.

The creature ignored its punctured chest — a wound that should have put it down, forevermore. It lunged after the gnome.

It crashed atop him.

It held him under.

Black claws slashed Ob's jerkin. Black, broken teeth gnashed, and strained to get at his throat.

Ob could barely see. The foul water stung his eyes like acid. He forced them wide; to hell with the pain. He reached out with his left hand. He grabbed the thing's neck. He had to hold it back. Had to keep those teeth at bay. His lungs burned. He needed air. He needed help.

The thing flailed. And slashed. Its strength, beyond a man's — even one as big as it. Its teeth, relentless. But for his chainmail shirt, it would have torn Ob to the bone.

He tried, Ob did. Fought as hard as he ever

did. But he couldn't hold back the fiend. It was too big. It was too strong.

Its jaws opened inhumanly wide. And snapped closed, over and again. They inched closer. Ever closer. Another moment, and they'd close on Ob's face, and then he'd be done for.

Ob gathered what strength remained in him. He thrust once more with his blade. Half blind was that blow. Lungs burning. Strength sapped. Instinct and experience took over. Ob had plenty of both. He aimed for the thing's maw.

His blow was sound. His blow was true. The sword angled upward. It entered the creature's mouth. It sank deep through its palate. It skewered the thing's brain.

The ghoul immediately went limp in the water. Ob's lungs were afire. He pushed the creature away. It was so heavy, the stinking thing. He only had the strength to move it but for the buoyancy of the water. He leaped up and gasped for air when he broke the surface.

Sounds of battle assailed Ob's ears. A wild melee raged around the boat. Ob pulled his sword free of the creature's corpse. He spun about on his tiptoes and readied to defend himself even as he struggled to keep his mouth above the churning water. No other enemies came at him, thank the gods. The stench of the swamp water, the taste of it on his lips, made him cough and gag. That just let more water into his mouth. A few inches deeper and it might well have drowned him.

Not far away, Red Tybor fought like a madman, leaping about, his spear deadly accurate — its movements almost too fast to follow. Ob saw him thrust it clear through one creature's torso, the razored tip exiting its back.

Steps away, Malvegil roared and cursed as he swung his great sword at a group of creatures that assailed him; his weapons master, Gorlick, on one side of him, and Gorlick's lieutenant, Karktan, on the other. Outnumbered three to one, they were hard pressed, but they were experts. The best of the best. One way or another, Ob knew, they'd beat the creatures back.

Ob couldn't see the others. Not clearly. Only shadowy figures fighting in the mist. He tried to get his bearings, but the darned vapors obscured everything. He saw the longboat — one end of it anyway, but only because it was just a few yards away. He knew that he had to get to it; that he had to get out of the water, or else risk some subsurface lurker pulling him down and tearing him to bits. He didn't want to end up like Rorbit.

He bobbed his way to the boat as fast as he could, coughing and spitting all the way. He grabbed the gunwale and tried to pull himself over the side. His soaked clothes and heavy armor weighed him down. He couldn't make it. He was vulnerable in that position; they could get at him from behind.

A quick glance back revealed nothing near, thank the gods. He tried again to scramble up, but failed.

Then Brother Donnelin reached over the side and hauled him up and over the rail. Good old Donnelin. He wasn't always useful, but when he was, he was.

Only Donnelin, Par Talbon, and stinking McDuff remained in the boat; the rest, Gabriel included, either fell, leaped, or had been pulled into the water.

The tip of Talbon's staff was aglow. Ob cringed; he had a sense of what was coming. He wanted to cover his ears, but he needed to keep hold of his sword. There wasn't anything he could duck behind, but he braced himself as best he could.

Fiery red spheres shot from the tip of Talbon's staff into the mist, one after another after another, at this angle and that, a loud "whooshing" sound accompanying each. How many he launched, Ob couldn't say for certain, perhaps fifteen, perhaps twenty.

The spheres exploded when they hit whatever they hit within the mist. Ob couldn't tell if they struck any of the creatures or not. Maybe the wizard knew. Maybe he could see through the murk with some weird wizard sight. Or maybe he was firing blind. Or maybe he was just shooting blanks. Ob didn't know. He didn't have much use for magic, since most of it was bunk, but if it did them some good in a tight spot like they were in, he'd suffer it.

McDuff was at the other end of the longboat fighting a ghoul that had somehow gotten aboard. The dwarf had a smile on his face. He liked battle a bit too much, that one did. With a single mighty slash of his battle axe, Ob saw him cut the thing clean in two at the waist. Its top half fell into the water; the bottom, dropped to the boat's deck. It should have gushed blood for a second or two at least, but there was nothing. No lifeblood flowed from that thing. How that could be, Ob didn't understand, for every living thing had blood coursing through its veins from the moment it was born until the moment it died. Some creatures had more blood than others, but large animals and men always had plenty. No exceptions to that as far as Ob had ever heard. So it meant one thing. The creature was dead before McDuff cut it down. How that could be, Ob didn't know. How could a dead man walk? How could he fight? How could he hunger? A chill went down Ob's spine. Black sorcery it must be.

The dark magic of Helheim.

Then Ob spotted Gabriel. He was in the water just beyond the boat's bow. Several creatures came at him, howling, all claws and teeth. His sword moved faster than Ob could follow. His movements even made Red Tybor's seem slow. He spun and dodged. Each swipe of his blade took off an arm or a leg or a head. He didn't tire. He didn't slow. He was unstoppable.

Off to the stern, Lord Aradon Eotrus cleaved through a creature's head with an overhand slash of his sword, and then went after another that lumbered nearby. Aradon favored a wide, thick blade, not as long as some, but very heavy. It made for a good weapon against the creatures. And he had no trouble wielding it. Hell, his arms were bigger around than most men's legs, yet he moved fluidly and swiftly. Lord or no, he was right there in the thick of it with the men and that made Ob proud. Proud to serve him. Proud to call him friend. A worthy lord he was. For that and many reasons.

Artol, a towering youth of mail and muscles, fought just a few feet away from Aradon. He crushed one creature's head and then another with a big battle hammer. Then he looked around for more. Gabriel had trained that fellow up good. Barely old enough to grow a beard, but a fearsome opponent was he.

Ob wanted to get back into it. To help his comrades. But the water was just too deep for him. And in any case, his boys were winning.

A few moments more and the battle was over. Most of the torn dead sank beneath the bog's inky surface, but some few floated, heads staved in or cut off, dismembered limbs bobbing here and there. A gruesome scene of death.

# 6

# DOR MALVEGIL

*Year 1242, Fourth Age
Twelfth Year of King Tenzivel's Rule*

Torbin Malvegil leaned against the balustrade on the fourth floor terrace. From there, he enjoyed a clear view of the town far below at the base of the cliff, and of the great river beyond, the Grand Hudsar. He could see for miles upriver and down, for Dor Malvegil stood high on an escarpment.

He enjoyed the terrace's view; never tired of it. His favorite spot it was, save for perhaps his study — where he kept his books, maps, and the mementos and heirlooms passed down from his forefathers and gathered during his own travels.

He was usually content when he stood on that terrace. But that morning, his jaw was set; his brow, furrowed.

He watched the schooner pull into port from downriver. A common sight, for Dor Malvegil boasted a busy river port, the source of much of his House's wealth. But then he saw men jump off the ship to confer with the harbormaster. He watched as the harbormaster's boy ran up the hill and jumped on one of the hoists, all nervous energy and excitement. He rode the hoist up to the top of the crag.

A message for the Malvegils is what he carried. Something important; something that couldn't wait. Grave news, it had to be, just as Landolyn predicted.

But what?

What news might come from the south? What danger lurked there?

"My lord," said Gravemare (Dor Malvegil's castellan) as he approached his lord on the terrace several minutes later. The captain of the schooner was with him. "May we speak with you for a moment? There is—"

"Another ship has gone missing," said Malvegil, though he did not turn toward them as he spoke.

"My lord?" said Gravemare. "How—"

"I am the great lord of the Malvegils," he said, his voice booming, and then turned toward them. His eyes fixed on the captain. "There is little that escapes my notice. Especially not three ships lost so near my borders in as many weeks." He marched up to the captain, his steely gaze boring into the man. The captain grew pale and looked ready to bolt. "You're a Lindener, aren't you?" he said. "Did Lady Mirtise send you?"

"Yes to both, my lord," he said, the captain's voice unsteady with nerves. "A man washed up in Dor Linden's bay. He floated downriver to us in a dinghy, he did. Was a Lomerian by his accent; a ship's cook by his garb. Delirious with fever, he was. Died soon after we found him. He babbled before he passed, but little of it made sense. Said his ship was attacked in the night as they passed by the Fens."

"Attacked by who?" said Malvegil.

"He didn't know; never saw them clearly. He

heard the fighting while he was below deck. They took folks prisoner and killed whoever resisted. Must have been pirates, though it be long years since any such plagued us this far north. He went overboard to escape, the cook did. He swam to shore but got jumped. They tore up his shoulder but good. A strange wound it was— more like a bite than a weapon cut. Saw it myself, I did."

"He ran for it, found an old dinghy, and drifted downriver. The wound festered along the way. Leren Jrack tried some things, but the cook was done for; died within hours. The Leren had his corpse burned to ash right quick, for fear of whatever done him in spreading to anyone else."

"What was the name of his ship?" said Malvegil.

"*The Bellowing Banshee*, out of Kern," said the captain. "Two or three dozen folk aboard. It was hard to get even that much out of him; his mind was gone; burned out from fever."

"I don't know that ship," said Malvegil.

"Nor did we," said the captain.

"No barge was it; not with that many aboard," said Malvegil.

"Maybe they're not after cargo," said Gravemare. "Maybe it's people they're after."

"Ransom?" said Malvegil.

"That or they're slavers up from Tragoss Mor," said Gravemare.

"Pirates or slavers?" said Malvegil. "I will suffer neither on my borders. I will see them dead, one and all."

"You will send a troop to hunt them down?" said Gravemare.

"I will hunt them down," said Malvegil. "It has been too long since I put my sword to proper use."

# 7

# DOR EOTRUS

*Year 1242, Fourth Age*
*Twelfth Year of King Tenzivel's Rule*

"**A** raven from Dor Malvegil, my Lord," said Pontly, Dor Eotrus's elderly castellan. He handed the missive to Aradon Eotrus, tall, thick, and rugged, his face pockmarked and mustached, his hair, black and close-cropped.

Aradon studied it. He read it twice without looking up.

Pontly shifted from one foot to the other, anxious to know what the note said, but unwilling to ask.

"Assemble a troop of heavy horse," said Aradon. "Three squadrons. We ride for Dor Malvegil on the morrow."

"What has happened, my lord?"

Aradon smiled. "My brother-in-law has invited us to go pirate hunting."

# 8

# THE DEAD FENS

*Year 1242, Fourth Age
Twelfth Year of King Tenzivel's Rule*

The battle around the longboat over, the Fen went quiet again, which made Ob all the more wary. The insects and such were still in hiding. The reptiles, the fish, all fled or else silent and still. All that buzzing and popping and croaking — all the natural sounds of the bog were gone.

All the sounds of life were gone.

Silence and the heavy breathing of battle weary men were all that remained.

Ob feared that meant there were more ghouls about. They'd weathered this wave, though not unscathed. Malvegil's wizard, Par Rorbit was missing, though that was no surprise to Ob after he'd seen him pulled under.

The Malvegils were not quick to give up on one of their own, however slight the chance that he might still live. They searched the water and called out Rorbit's name. Perhaps he was alive, out there, hidden by the mist. The longboat had moved a ways during the battle, drifting with the turbulence of the battle and the tidal flows that influenced the water. It was not impossible that Rorbit had surfaced injured, and pulled himself up on a mudbank or floating debris somewhere about the battle's perimeter.

"Malvegil should've kept his sorcerer at home," whispered Artol to Ob. "They're no warriors."

"That one was, same as Talbon," whispered Ob. "A war wizard of the Red Tower, Rorbit was, and a knife fighter to boot. As good with a short blade as Stern, I'd wager. A fell day this is, losing him."

"I figured Rorbit for a hedge," said Artol.

Ob chuckled. "Malvegil would never suffer a hedge wizard in his court. He's got little patience for fools or charlatans."

"I don't care much for wizards myself," said Ob, "but Rorbit was one of the few what earned my respect. Fought with us in some campaigns up north, he did, years back, when you was but a pup. A tough bugger. He'll be missed."

"Did any escape us?" asked Gabriel as he peered about into the haze and flicked his sword to knock off the clinging gore.

"None tried," said McDuff the Mighty, a wide-shouldered dwarf of bulging muscles and glinty golden armor that he made himself. An old friend of Malvegil's was he.

"He's right," said Malvegil as he waded through the water, searching. "They came on to the last. Like mad dogs with no regard for their own lives."

"What courage to leap at us even as we cut down their brethren," said Karktan, a tall, burly, bearded Malvegil man that looked much like his lord, only younger and larger. Like most of the others, Karktan shivered from the cold, his clothes drenched, though he voiced no complaint about it.

"Waste not your respect on them, Volsung," said Red Tybor, a bronze savage with black eyes and a dot of long hair atop his otherwise clean-shaven head. "Hunger or madness drove them, not courage. These were not men."

Ob cast the Pict a look as if to say, *you would know.*

"Then what were they?" said Artol.

Red Tybor shook his head.

"He's gone, Torbin," said Master Gorlick, a chiseled veteran of steely eyes and lean muscle, as he waded through the putrid water beside his liege. "My lord—"

"I know he's gone, dammit," shouted Malvegil. "Do you think me daft?" Malvegil reached out and grabbed Gorlick about the shoulder. Malvegil's eyes glistened. "I need to bring him home. For his wife, his children. I can't just leave him out here to rot. They need to bury him. To say their goodbyes. Keep looking, all of you. And keep your teeth together."

No one said anything more as the Malvegils continued to search the water, and the Eotrus men kept watch. After a time, unsuccessful, Malvegil made his way back to the longboat, his men helping him in. He stood tall in the boat and got the attention of all the men. "Even caught by surprise, by cowardly ambush, it took two of them things to pull Rorbit into the bog," said Malvegil in his booming voice, anguish on his face. "And he gave them what for, he did. Took them things with him, he did."

"It's true," said Gorlick as he wrapped a cloth about his arm, injured in the fight. "A warrior's death he had, my lord. He took a dozen of the things with him, maybe more," Gorlick said, pointing to the body parts afloat in the water. "If not for that, a much tougher fight for us it would have been. His place in Valhalla is assured."

"What killed him?" said Malvegil. "What in Odin's name were those things?"

"To my eyes," said Gorlick, "they looked like dead men. Like corpses come back to life."

"You tell us what they were," said Ob to Malvegil. "We came here on your request — to fight pirates, not dead men what walk. What have you gotten us into, Malvegil? What haven't you told us?"

"I didn't know about these creatures," said Malvegil. "I told you all I knew before we left my Dor."

Brother Donnelin, House Cleric for the Eotrus, picked his way to Gorlick's side and helped him bind up his bleeding arm, as did Gorlick's young aid, Karktan of Rivenwood.

"They were not men," said Donnelin as he knelt beside Gorlick, working on his wound. "Fiends of the pit. Ghouls out of Helheim they were."

"Don't start spouting fairy stories, you stinking windbag," said Ob. "There's no such thing as ghouls."

"My arm disputes that," said Gorlick.

Ob stared at him blankly.

"In elder days, ghouls did roam the dark places of Midgaard," said Gabriel. "But these were not ghouls. They were something else. Something different. Something that I haven't seen before."

"I've seen dead men pulled from the water what looked as these," said McDuff. "All bloated and rotting."

"Dead men don't walk," said Artol. "And they don't fight."

"When the dead walk, Helheim be full," said Red Tybor. His words sent a chill over them all. "So goes a legend of my people, carried down from olden days. Every Pictish child knows it."

"Nothing but rubbish," said Ob.

"There is dark sorcery at work here," said Par Talbon, a short, slight Eotrus man of jet-black hair, dressed to match. "I can feel it," he said as he clutched his wizarding staff. "We must be wary."

"A necromancer?" said Gabriel.

"Mayhap," said Talbon. "Or a chaos sorcerer."

"A what?" said Malvegil. "Speak plainly, wizard."

"A necromancer is a wizard that can summon or command the dead," said Talbon. "A chaos sorcerer is a practitioner of the dark arts. Both types draw their power from the nether realms — Nifleheim, Helheim, or the like, instead of the magical weave."

"How can that be?" said Malvegil. "I thought the weave was the source of all magic."

"Not according to the chaos sorcerers," said Talbon.

"And here we are, down one wizard," said Artol.

"We've still got one what's serviceable," said Ob, eyeing Talbon. "Two, if you count the windbag priest," he said of Donnelin.

Malvegil's eyes still scanned the water. He looked ready to jump back in and continue his search.

Aradon Eotrus grasped his shoulder. "He is gone," said Aradon. "There is naught that you can do for him. And we can linger here no longer."

"He's an archwizard, for Odin's sake," said Malvegil, his voice quiet again.

"Even the great may fall in battle," said Aradon. "That's the way of things. No one is immune to death. We must accept this and move on. Our mission remains."

"I care not to leave my men behind," said Malvegil.

"Nor do I," said Aradon, "but sometimes we must."

"What now?" said McDuff, his thick red beard extending into his lap.

"We cannot linger here," said Red Tybor. "Too much talk already."

Gabriel moved close to them and spoke quietly. "Red Tybor is right; we have lingered here too long already. We should move on at once. More of them may yet come, attracted to the sounds of the battle."

"You think that there are more?" said Malvegil. "But what are they, truly? They cannot be dead men. I won't believe that."

"Perhaps they are lepers of some kind," said Gabriel. "Or perhaps some other wasting disease afflicts them, mind and body. I know not. We'll figure it out later. But now, we must move."

"But do we go forward or back?" said Aradon.

"Back, my lords," said Brother Donnelin, having overheard them since neither Eotrus nor Malvegil had any skill at whispering. "If there are more of those creatures about, we will need more men and more longboats or else we risk getting trapped and overrun."

"If we are to rescue any survivors from the missing ship," said Gabriel, "we must go forward now. We don't have time to go back for reinforcements. We must see this through with those few we have."

His aspect grave, Malvegil nodded and took his seat.

"On your oars," said Gabriel. "We're moving. Into the deeps. We'll change into dry clothes as soon as we find dry land. In the meantime, we'll keep warm by working up a sweat."

Malvegil scowled and turned to Aradon. "It's not Gabriel's place to issue orders here," he whispered. "Get your man in line."

"Not I," said Aradon. "Gabriel cannot be tamed."

Malvegil looked shocked at Eotrus's response. "Does he work for you or not?"

"No. Not in the way that you mean. Gabriel is his own man, always has been. He's a friend, but has sworn no fealty to me or to any lord. And I doubt that he ever would. But that doesn't matter. He knows things, Torbin; many things. Best to put your ego aside when he's around. When trouble shows its face, let him take the reins now and again. You'll do the better for it."

"To Helheim with that," said Malvegil. "I never expected to hear the like from you." He raised his voice so that all the men could hear him. "Row ahead and let's find us some solid ground. Keep silent and keep alert."

"You heard Lord Malvegil, men," said Aradon.

"Let's move."

"Landolyn was right, as always," muttered Malvegil to Aradon. "She said I would regret this quest; that I should let the Fens be. Let Lomion City protect its ships, she told me. I should have listened."

"Why did she tell us only twelve must go?" said Aradon. "And why did you listen? If we had come with all the men that I brought down from the North, and as many of your own, these things would be no threat to us."

"I don't know why," said Malvegil. "I don't understand her magic, her prophecies. Perhaps the Norns guide her; perhaps it's something else. I know not. But I trust her. Twelve men and twelve only, she said. Six Malvegils and six Eotrus, and no more. Why it must be thus, I cannot say, but I trust her."

They rowed on in haste for some minutes, their mood, grim.

Donnelin tried to convince the lords to turn back, but they would not listen.

After a time, they spied a large shadow looming in the mist up ahead. They approached it slowly, with caution, and as quietly as they could.

A ship.

It was a ship run aground.

# 9

# DOR EOTRUS LORD EOTRUS'S PRIVATE QUARTERS

*Year 1242, Fourth Age
Twelfth Year of King Tenzivel's Rule*

"**I** know that you're planning to divorce me," said Lady Eleanor Eotrus in a serious tone devoid of emotion.

"What?" spat Aradon as he brushed the crust from his eyes. He was half-asleep and wasn't certain that he heard her right. What was she doing up so early? "What are you talking about, woman?"

His wife stood at the foot of the bed, her hair done, makeup on. She wore a low-cut attractive dress; one that he favored. He could barely see straight, the sleep still in his eyes, but she was a vision of beauty, as always. Every time he looked at her, it took his breath away.

He looked toward the window. It was just past dawn.

"It's been five years and I haven't given you an heir," said Eleanor. "Not one son; not one daughter. Nothing. I'm barren, worthless. I've failed you. I've failed as a wife, as a woman. I'm useless."

Aradon sat up at the edge of the bed. He saw

Eleanor's travel bags by the bedroom door, stuffed to bursting.

Aradon stood, his bare arms huge with muscles. His handlebar mustache disheveled from sleep. He saw that it was all she could do not to burst out crying. That wasn't like her. She was a level-headed woman. That was one of the qualities he most admired in her.

He stepped toward her, but she flinched back and looked down. "My mind is made up," she said. "I'm going back to Dor Malvegil. I will sign whatever papers that are necessary from there. I will ask nothing of you. Nothing at all, save that you send me any of my things that I have forgotten. My brother will see to my needs henceforth. I will not return. You will be free of me. Free to find a more suitable wife. One that will give you the children that you deserve."

He moved toward her, to embrace her, but she stepped back and put up her hand. "No! It is done. Do not touch me. Never again."

Aradon grabbed her hand in a grip that she could not hope to resist. "You are my wife," he said, his voice stern and strong. Then his voice grew tenderer. "And you are not going anywhere. I love you."

"Aradon, no," she said. "I know that you love me. And I, you. That's not what this is about. It's about House Eotrus. It's your responsibility to carry on the family line. You have no siblings. It all falls to you. And I cannot bear you an heir. You must divorce me. You must wed another that can give you an heir and carry on the family line. It's not about what you and I want. It's about the good of the House. We must do this."

"I am the Lord of Dor Eotrus," said Aradon in the same commanding voice he used when holding court. "And I will decide these matters. Not you. Not anyone else."

"Do you think that I haven't thought about the need for an heir?" he said. "Do you think I'm unaware of my responsibilities?"

"I know you've thought of it," said Eleanor. "Just as I know that you've been planning to divorce me. But you're too good hearted to tell me. You've been putting it off for too long. Far too long. The longer this goes on, the harder it will be for the both of us. That's why I'm leaving. That's why I brought this up. I'm trying to make it easier on you. On us. I know what has to be done. And I'm doing it."

"Don't you see that it has to be this way?" said Eleanor. "I can't live every day wondering if today is the day that you're going to tell me. If today is the day our life together is over. I can't take it. The stress of that. I can't live like that. I have to go on my own terms. I have to go now. Today."

"I understand," he said. He pointed to the couch in the sitting area and they both sat down. Eleanor looked defeated. All the strength gone from her body.

"I didn't know that you had these fears," said Aradon. "I'm sorry. I should have known. I should have been more observant."

"You've done nothing wrong," she said. "You're governing the House as is your duty."

"And what is the House without my wife? Servants, soldiers, and stone. That's all."

"You will have another wife. One that isn't broken," she said, holding back sobs. "Then you will have many children and this place will be full of laughter and happiness, as it should be."

"We should have had this conversation long ago," said Aradon. "What a fool I've been. I hoped that you would be with child and that we'd never have to discuss this. So I put it off. That was a mistake."

"I'm not afraid of anything," said Aradon, "yet, I was afraid to discuss these things with you. And for that, I'm truly sorry. Had I understood the pain it was causing you, I would have brought it up long ago."

"Don't blame yourself," she said, her voice breaking up. "It's all my fault. You've been a good husband. Too good for me."

"When we stood in the Odinhome and took our vows before the gods, I promised to love you and be faithful to you forevermore," said Aradon. "I did not take those words lightly at the time, nor do I now. You are my wife. And you will remain so for as long as we both walk Midgaard."

"What?" she said, whimpering.

"If the Eotrus line is to have no heir," said Aradon, "then we will have no heir. It falls to the will of the gods."

Eleanor looked shocked. Her mouth was open, but no words tumbled out.

"You are still very young, my love," he said. "The gods may yet favor us with children. But if they don't, they don't. I will not forsake you. I will not forsake the vows that I have made. Not for anything. Nor will I allow you to do so to try to protect the House."

"I will never leave you, Eleanor. Not now. Not ever. Unpack your bags now, or I'll throw them on the hearth."

Eleanor's mouth was moving, but still no words came out. Tears streamed down her cheeks, her face all flushed.

"Do as I say, woman."

She fell to her knees and clutched at his leg. "You're not?" she said. "You're not going to leave me? Not going to cast me aside?"

"Never," said Aradon as he scooped her up in his arms and held her close. "Not for all the riches in Midgaard."

# 10

# THE DEAD FENS

*Year 1242, Fourth Age*
*Twelfth Year of King Tenzivel's Rule*

**W**hen the longboat drew close enough, the mist parted to reveal a small caravel, typical of those owned by Lomerian nobles and wealthy merchants. The ship was run aground into a bank of mud. Dry land (as dry as the Fens offered) lay beyond. No one appeared to be about.

Surprised expressions filled the men's faces.

"How did they ever get a vessel that big this far into the deeps?" said Malvegil. "We've barely made it with the longboat."

"Dumb luck," said Ob. "Or else, the pilot knew the Fens far better than we."

"The latter, I'd wager," said Gabriel. "Chance did not bring it here."

Malvegil got Red Tybor's attention and gestured with his head. As they approached the shore, Red Tybor leaped from the longboat with agility that few men on Midgaard could match. He circled the caravel, sniffing the air as he went, his eyes darting this way and that all the while. He studied the ground around the boat, and then pulled himself up and over its rail with as little effort as most men expended walking up a stair. He walked about the deck, silent as stone, then crouched down and disappeared from sight.

The others kept their places in the longboat and waited, keeping watch; those who were still wet, shivered, though none complained. More than one of them looked time and again at the water. They checked for any disturbance, any ripple that might hint that more of the creatures lurked down there, beneath the water's surface, watching, waiting, readying to pounce on them.

But there was nothing. No sign of them; those things. No trace. A minute or two passed with no sign or signal from Red Tybor.

"Where is he?" said Artol.

"He could be in trouble," said Brother Donnelin. "Maybe there are more creatures on that ship."

Malvegil moved his arm and hand, gesturing silence. "Keep still and keep quiet," he said in a tone that brooked no opposition.

Soon, Red Tybor's head appeared over the rail.

"It's clear," he said. "Several died in battle aboard within a ten day."

"Bodies?" said Gabriel.

Red Tybor shook his head. "Stains only. They had women and children with them."

"Dead gods," said Malvegil. "Women and children? Now there's all the more urgency to our quest. What track or trail? Which way do we go?"

Red Tybor leaped over the rail and landed lightly beside the caravel. He squatted and studied the ground. The others took the opportunity to change into dry clothes. Then they gathered their equipment and disembarked. Ob moved to the Pict's side.

"Rain has come twice in the last ten day, once

heavy," said Red Tybor. "And the tide has rolled over this ground each day, first in, then out. There is nothing left to follow. Not a trace."

Ob studied the ground around the caravel for some minutes and then reported his findings. "As the stinking Pict said, there is no clear trail, but there are small signs that they may have headed toward the southeast. Besides, the land is drier in that direction. If I was going to set up base in these parts, that's the way I'd go."

"How certain are you that they went that way?" said Aradon.

"An educated guess is all," said Ob. "But that's the best we've got, so I suggest that we get going, while the going is good."

"A guess is not good enough," said Malvegil. "We have to be certain. Lives are on the line. If we head the wrong way now, we may not find the captives in time."

"You still think to find them alive after what we just went through?" said Ob.

"We don't know that it was those creatures that attacked the caravel," said Malvegil.

"If it was—" said Ob.

"If it was, they're dead," said Malvegil. "And we'll avenge them as best we can. Mayhap we already have. Those we killed may be all of them. But if someone else took the boat, there may yet be captives to free."

"How likely is it that another force, pirates or otherwise, is operating in these Fens without your knowledge?" said Ob.

"I intend to see this through," said Malvegil. "Are you with me or not?"

Aradon spoke up before Ob answered. "We are with you," he said and then turned toward Gabriel. "Can your token find us a trail?"

"Perhaps," said Gabriel. He grasped the ankh in his right hand and intently peered at it. That strange token was sorely battered and bruised. A slash from some blade had cut halfway through it, and charred edges bespoke of a fire that near consumed it in the distant past. It looked old. Ancient. As old or older than any craft of man.

"Must we bother with this mummery?" said Ob. Looking to the others, he said, "Every time we don't know which way to go, he pulls out that thingamabob. As if a stinking piece of gnarled old wood or stone, or whatever it's made of, knew something about something. It doesn't work, that thing. How could it? He just picks a direction, whichever he fancies, and off we go, as if Odin himself decreed it. Are we sheep? Are we stinking lemmings? Who does he think he's fooling, anyways? Waste of our stinking time is all it is. Southeast is as good as any direction, and better than most. I say that we head that way a while and see what there is to see. Mayhap when we get past the tide line there will even be some trail that we can follow. We can always double back if we don't find anything."

"Be not so quick to mock the old ways," said Red Tybor as he strung his bow. "My people have used tokens such as Gabriel's ankh from times beyond memory."

"Your people live in straw and mud huts in the stinking wastelands, and sleep with your stinking cattle, except when you're cuddling up to your goats," said Ob. "So I don't much care what your people think about anything."

Red Tybor merely rolled his eyes at Ob's barbs, though the same words bespoken by one he didn't call friend may have cost the speaker his life.

"No offense to any, but I prefer to rely on the true gods who watch over us each day of our lives," said Brother Donnelin. He produced a leather pouch, cleared a dry area on the ground, knelt down, and upended the pouch with a flourish. The men gathered around to watch. A goodly number of small gray-white stones of various shapes tumbled out of his pouch, falling atop one another. Each one had strange markings carved into it. "Through the grace of Lord Odin and all the mighty Aesir, the rune stones will show us the way."

"Humbug, bunk, and bother," said Ob as he pushed his hands against his head, momentarily covering his eyes. "For Odin's sake, trust in your brains, your brawn, and your blades, not some useless bits of rock. You'll get nothing from them but dust on your hands. They're as bad and foolish as Gabe's whatchamacallit. Fools you are, one and all. Simpletons. Superstitious morons."

Brother Donnelin bent low over the rune stones and studied them carefully, intently. Every few seconds he glanced for the merest moment at Gabriel who still stared at his ankh and waved it about.

"Our path lies that way," said Gabriel, pointing toward the southeast.

"The rune stones agree," said Donnelin confidently. "To the southeast we must go to meet our destiny. The gods have decreed it."

"Ready your gear," said Gabriel. "We move out in five minutes."

"Southeast," said Artol to Ob as he pointed in that direction. "It looks drier that way, doesn't it?"

"Are you kidding me?" said Ob. "Does no one listen to me? No one at all?"

No one answered.

Malvegil moved to Gorlick's side. "Master Gorlick, are you well enough to continue?" As Gorlick started to respond, Malvegil held his palm out to stop him. "On your honor, I command you to speak true. I care not to lose you too."

"It's little more than a scratch, my lord," said Gorlick, "though it hurts more than it should. I've had worse a dozen times at least. If it hadn't bled so much, I would not have even mentioned it. I will see this through. Besides, I suspect you'll need my sword again before this quest is done."

"I fear I will," said Malvegil. "But I'm glad that you're with us, for there is no finer swordsman in all Lomion."

**T**hankfully, they left the thickest fog behind at the water's edge. Beyond, over the deeps of the Fens, lay only a murky haze that hung a few inches to as high as a few feet above the wet ground for as far as they could see in all directions. A putrid miasma permeated the place – a sweet and sour scent of death and decay, of rotting plants and such. The mosquitoes were thick and hungry, undeterred by the unseasonably cold weather. And the place was eerily quiet – no chirping bird or insect, no croaking frog or slithering serpent hissed or wild monkey howled. It was as quiet as a tomb.

# 11

# THE DEAD FENS

*Year 1242, Fourth Age*
*Twelfth Year of King Tenzivel's Rule*

The trek through the swampy expanse was a trial for them all, but especially difficult for the dwarf, McDuff, and for Ob, due to their short statures. The group moved forward in single file at what was an agonizingly slow pace for men of action, but necessary due to the treacherous footing afforded by the ever-present haze and uneven swampy ground. The mud sucked at their legs like a living beast trying to pull them down into the earth. Time and again, the bog tried to steal their boots, gripping them so hard they tripped or their feet pulled clear out of them. That slowed them down even more, as they had to stop and fish their shoes out; a swamp, even the drier parts of it, was nowhere to travel barefoot.

With Rorbit's loss, eleven men remained. Red Tybor, Pictish bow in hand, traveled at the van, some distance ahead of the others. Then went Sir Gabriel, Artol, Par Talbon, Lord Aradon Eotrus, Lord Torbin Malvegil, McDuff the Mighty, Master Gorlick, Karktan of Rivenwood, and Brother Donnelin, with Ob covering the rear. Soldiers all, most of long experience. But despite all their skills and efforts, they created a veritable cacophony as they made their way through the muck. There was just no way to pass over that ground in silence. Even Red Tybor's passage made noise. Not much. But too much for his liking, for he normally moved as quietly as a mouse.

"They'll hear us coming from a league away," grumbled Ob. "Stinking big folk." Though in truth, he wasn't making much less noise than most of the others.

"You are troubled?" said Eotrus to Malvegil as they trudged along.

Malvegil hesitated before speaking, seeming to decide whether he should speak at all. "How can I face Rorbit's family? I've known Clara for ten years, and his children all their lives. Not only did I get him killed, but I can't even bring his body home to them. How can I face them? If this had happened in war, with a horde of Lugron coming out of the wild, it would be different. But now, when things have been peaceful for years..."

"Peaceful down here, perhaps," said Aradon. "We've had our troubles in the North in recent times, as you well know. Leading men into battle be no easy task, my friend, for even victory brings its burdens and its pains. Fear not, for you will find the strength you need to face them, just as you found the strength needed to face those creatures in battle."

Malvegil didn't look convinced.

"There will be time enough for reflection and for grieving later, Torbin. Think not again on this until we march on the homeward road. Keep your mind focused on the present and the tasks at hand. Don't let your thoughts stray for even a moment or in peril you will be."

"Wise words," Malvegil said with a hint of his customary grin. "I'll heed them as best I can. I'm glad to have you with me in this."

They walked uneventfully through the bog for the rest of the day. Gabriel periodically used his ankh to check and correct their course; Ob grumbled and scoffed each time he pulled it out. The haze thickened and thinned, and rose and sank at random as they made their way. They stopped only when they began to lose the light, for traveling at night in the Fens was far too dangerous, and they could not risk lighting torches for fear of giving away their presence and position. They set up camp on a drier patch of land in an area with more foliage than most, the better to hide them from sight. No fire dared they light, making it a cold night indeed.

# 12

# DOR EOTRUS THE LORD'S PRIVATE DINING ROOM

*Year 1242, Fourth Age
Twelfth Year of King Tenzivel's Rule*

"I'm not going to let House Eotrus fall because of me," said Eleanor as she and her husband sat across the dining table from each other.

Aradon froze, his fork suspended over his dinner; the breath caught in his throat. He had thought they put this behind them. "Are you talking about an heir again?"

She nodded.

"We settled this last week."

"We didn't," she said. "Not really. All we settled was that you love me too much to give me up. You're a good husband; a great husband. But you have responsibilities as the lord of the House. Those responsibilities are far more important than me. Than us."

"The Eotrus have been the shining light of the North for hundreds of years," she said. "Without this House, all of the northern lands would have long ago been overrun. Lomion City itself may have fallen; the world turned on its head. Dor Malvegil would have fallen soon after. I cannot be the cause of the line of Eotrus coming to an end.

I will not be. This House is just too important."

"We may yet have children," said Aradon. "You are only twenty-three, for Odin's sake. There are many years left."

"And you are forty. And a soldier. You live a dangerous life. You take many risks. What if something happens to you while we're still trying?"

"There is no other solution that I will entertain," said Aradon.

"One year."

"What are you saying?"

"We will try for one more year. If by the end of that time I am not with child, you will give me up and find another."

"It may not even be you that is the problem," said Aradon. "Mayhap there is something wrong with me that prevents it."

"I have never heard of such a thing," said Eleanor, "except when a man is grievously wounded there. You are whole. The only way to find out, is if you were to be with another woman and she were to conceive a child or not."

"Or for you to be with another man."

Eleanor looked shocked. "I would never . . ."

"As I said, there is no other solution that I will entertain."

"So you've thought all this through?" she said. "Of course you have. That is your way. You cannot have an illegitimate child. The complications—"

"Again, we don't disagree."

"One year only."

"No. It will not be that way. You are my wife and—"

71

"I will take matters into my own hands, if I must."

Aradon went silent. His face darkened. "What say you?"

"If after one more year of trying, I am not with child, you will divorce me, and I will return to Dor Malvegil. If you don't, I will do what must be done."

"You cannot divorce me," said Aradon. "As a Dor Lord, I am exempt from such—"

"That is not what I meant and you know it."

Aradon's voice grew weak. "What did you mean?"

"Don't make me say it. Please don't."

He didn't.

***

"You were right," said Eleanor. "I think it worked. If I'm not pregnant in a year, he will divorce me. He'd rather that than see me dead. I never would have thought of that on my own. You know him so well; I envy you that. You're a good friend to him."

"He is very happy with you," said Sir Gabriel. "Happier than I've seen him in many years. I truly wish that before the year is out you are with child, and that you two stay together for the rest of your days. I mean that."

"I know you do," said Eleanor. "You're a good friend to both of us. You're just trying to protect him, and protect House Eotrus. Aradon has let his love for me cloud his vision. As his wife, I love him for that. As Lady Eotrus, I cannot accept it. House Eotrus needs an heir. The family line must continue."

Gabriel nodded. "Indeed, it must."

# 13

# THE DEAD FENS

*Year 1242, Fourth Age*
*Twelfth Year of King Tenzivel's Rule*

It's a hard thing to sleep on the cold ground, no fire to warm you. Harder still when the ground is damp and the moisture wicks up your clothes; when you've no tent; when the creepy crawlies nibble at you all night long; when there are things out in the darkness that want to kill you dead.

But they were hard men, the Malvegils and the Eotrus. They were used to the wilds and the hardships and dangers that came with it. The Eotrus hailed from the northernmost region of the kingdom, at the edge of the wild, near the foothills of the Kronar Mountains — some of the tallest, coldest, and least explored peaks in the known world.

The Eotrus were warriors, born and bred. They'd weathered countless raids by Lugron, bandits, and barbarians, and more than one outright invasion. They'd fought many times against beasts that came down from the mountains with a taste for human flesh. Sometimes it was a wolf pack. Other times, a rogue bear, a mountain lion, or wild boars. Some of the worst were the sabre cats. They were huge, fast, and deadly, and all too often hunted in packs. Luckily, they didn't come down from the hills very often.

Going back several generations, the Malvegils were the Eotrus's closest ally amongst the great Houses of Lomerian nobility and had often taken to the field with them against the various threats that the North spewed forth. That alliance had grown all the closer five years previous when Aradon Eotrus wed Eleanor Malvegil, Torbin Malvegil's younger sister, though the union had yet to bear an heir.

The Eotrus and the Malvegils were amongst the most experienced and skilled warriors in the Kingdom of Lomion. Adventurers, mercenaries, and would-be heroes were attracted to their ranks, though unlike the Malvegils, the Eotrus rarely accepted southerners or foreigners into their fold. They preferred to mingle with and keep pure the olden Volsung bloodlines of the original settlers of the North. Some legends even claimed that the oldest Northern families were truly ancient indeed. That their lineage extended far back into prehistory, back beyond even The Age of Heroes, back even unto the Age of Myth and Legend, when the gods themselves strode across Midgaard, doing deeds and fighting mighty foes, as was their wont.

**B**etween the cold, the wet, the bugs, the death of Par Rorbit, and the notion of prowling dead men pouncing on them in the night, sleep didn't come easy. Most of the men were unusually talkative. Gorlick brooded, which wasn't like him. Ob could tell that his arm wound bothered him, though Gorlick was loath to admit it.

Ob passed Gorlick a wineskin, and spoke just loud enough to get the other men's attention. "Some might say that old Master Gorlick here has lost a step or two, getting his arm gnawed on by a shambling, uncoordinated dead thing. Now that would be a mistake. Artol, my boy, do you know what this surly bugger is good for?"

Artol shrugged.

"He's killed more Lugron than you've even seen," said Ob. "And I know that you've seen your share. He's put down sabre cats single handedly. Bunches of them through the years. He's taken enough of their skins to carpet your house twice over. Bears too. Now I'm not talking about them docile-as-dogs black bears what come around and nose through the garbage heap. I mean the huge cave bears, the brown and the gray ones. The ones what could gobble a grown man up for breakfast and still have room enough to eat two whole goats or sheep.

"Mountain lions have fallen to his swords. So have gators, dire wolves, and more. Over the last twenty years, most anything what came down from the mountains, or crawled out of some cave or bog within three hundred leagues of here, and was looking to harm innocent folks, — old Gorlick went out and faced it, and killed it dead."

"Don't forget the ogre," said Red Tybor.

"An ogre?" said Artol. "You fought an actual ogre?"

Gorlick nodded.

"I was getting to the ogre," said Ob. "Don't be so hasty, Pict boy. He was man-eating, that ogre. Giantish. Muscles on muscles. Eight feet tall, toe to temple."

"Nine feet," said Gorlick.

"Even dead, that stinking ogre grows bigger every year," said Ob. "Be ten feet tall by next winter, I expect. Old Gorlick killed it dead up in some cave out east, all by his lonesome, he did. The thing was raiding villages, making off with folks and eating them up. Not just children, mind you, but full-grown adults. Sometimes it took them from the streets at night. Sometimes from their own yards in the light of the day. Scooped them right up and carried them off never to be seen alive again."

"But what the evil bastard liked best, was to creep into homes in the dead of night and eat folks right in their own beds, the rest of the family asleep in other rooms, none the wiser. It left broken bones behind, the marrow sucked out. Not much else left. Bits of skin and hair. Barely could tell it was a person, if even."

"Gorlick put a stop to that killing, he did," said Ob. "Found that ogre's stinking lair and gave it what for, didn't you?"

"I did," said Gorlick. "A hard fight. Hard to keep the thing down."

"That's not how I heard it at all," said Red Tybor. All eyes turned toward the Pict. "I heard that Gorlick met up with the ogre's wife out in the woods and fell in love with her. And that she was the one what was nine feet tall."

The men laughed.

"That's not it," said Malvegil. "It was the ogre he fell in love with, and the ogress that attacked him for it in a fit of jealousy."

More laughter.

"He's a darned juggernaut, old Gorlick is," said Ob. "Got that ogre's head mounted on the wall in Dor Malvegil. Or maybe it's the ogress's head. Who could tell?"

"What's a juggernaut?" said Artol.

"Some kind of fruit?" said Red Tybor.

"It's something what can't be stopped by nothing," said Ob. "Something that will kill you dead no matter what you do to stop it. Some warriors got that kind of fire in them. Not many, mind you. Maybe one in ten thousand, if that. But them that got it can be great heroes if the opportunity presents and they've a mind to do it. Or else, they can be wretched villains. However be their nature."

"You calling Gorlick a villain?" said Red Tybor.

"Never," said Ob. "I'm calling him wretched."

More laughter.

"Anyways," said Ob, his tone becoming serious, "after killing all them big baddies and evil nasties and whatnot, and coming out with nary a scrape or even mussed hair, you think that old Gorlick went and let a stupid, shambling, falling apart piece of cat dung take a chunk out of his arm? I don't buy it. Not for one minute. I'll have the truth from you, Master Gorlick, and I'll have it now."

Gorlick didn't seem to know what to say.

"You can't fool an old gnome," said Ob. "I know exactly what you was up to. You shoved your arm into that thing's mouth on purpose. You figured that one bite out of your sour, surly flesh would poison it up good and kill it dead in an instant."

More laughter.

"You laugh," said Ob as he looked around at the men. "Tell me, where's that stinking thing now? The one what bit Gorlick?"

"Dead," said the Pict.

"So it worked," said Ob smiling.

"That was my plan exactly," said Gorlick, finally cracking a smile.

# 14

# THE DEAD FENS

*Year 1242, Fourth Age*
*Twelfth Year of King Tenzivel's Rule*

Malvegil awoke with a start. He'd heard something in his sleep.

A call? A scream? Or was it just a dream?

He opened his eyes and looked around, barely moving his head so as not to attract attention. The moons were waning, but the sky was clear, so it was hard to see, though not completely black.

Master Gorlick, who was closest to him, put a hand to his back. "Keep still and silent, my lord," he whispered.

Malvegil felt the tension in Gorlick's voice — he was rattled, maybe even afraid. And Gorlick feared nothing. Something was afoot. Something dangerous. Malvegil dared not move. But from where he lay, with the help of the moonlight, he saw that at least some of the others were awake, eyes open, listening, poised to rise, hands on weapons.

Then it came again, the sound that he'd heard in his sleep — a strange howl. Awake, he recognized it at once. It was the same sound he heard when those things attacked their longboat.

Now they knew for certain that there were more of them — the "shamblers," as they came to call them. And they were out there. In the black.

Roaming about. But was this another chance encounter? Or were the things tracking them? Hunting them? How many were out there?

Sounds traveled strangely in the bog, but Malvegil guessed that the howl came from within a hundred yards of their camp. That was too close for comfort. Especially, if there were a group of the things. If they had the men's scent, they'd be in the camp in moments. Fighting them in the light was hard enough; in the dark would be all the more deadly.

Hopefully, if they remained silent and still, they might go unnoticed. The shamblers might pass them by. Soon, Malvegil smelled them. A putrid scent of rotted, decaying flesh, akin to a week-old battlefield. He put a hand to his sword hilt and made ready to draw it should a shambler creep out of the night into camp.

Then Malvegil heard a hissing sound. It grew louder by the moment. A sound akin to a snake, but much too loud to be one. He turned his head, and spotted the true cause of Gorlick's stress. Not five yards away was the largest snake that Malvegil had ever seen.

It was slithering through their camp, its forked tongue, two feet long, flicking this way and that. A swamp python it looked like, its skin a mottled beige and brown, but massive — two feet around, with a head much larger than a man's. How long it was, he could only guess, since much of its body was hidden by the night, but surely, its span was more than forty feet.

More howls from the shamblers cut through the night air. Closer now were they, and drawing still closer by the moment. From the sounds, there had to be at least a dozen of the things. Maybe a score.

The snake seemed agitated by the howling, reacting by bobbing its head and changing its course each time the howls filled the air. It was clear enough; the snake wanted no part of the shamblers.

Malvegil wondered how they could deal with the snake without giving away their position to the shamblers. If they had to fight both at the same time, it might well be a disaster.

The snake was moving in Malvegil's direction. Malvegil's heart pounded in his chest. The hair stood up on the back of his neck. He needed to get up. Pull out his sword. Slay the thing. Or die in the trying.

Or else, run for it.

The last thing he wanted to do is lay there motionless, doing nothing; hiding like a scared rabbit. He was a man of action. Such was against his nature.

But lay there he had too, or else attract the attention of the shamblers. Since he didn't know their numbers, he couldn't chance that. He wouldn't. It might get more of his men killed.

Gorlick was still behind him. Malvegil felt his tension too; he could tell by his breathing. The weapons master was coiled, ready to spring.

The snake stopped. Its forked tongue zipped in and out of its mouth, vibrating so quickly that it hummed. Then it moved within two feet of Ob, who appeared fast asleep, his eyes closed, his breathing shallow. Malvegil was sure that the crusty old bastard was done for. If that thing struck him, the little man wouldn't stand a chance. The snake was more than big enough to swallow him whole. And no doubt, it could easily crush the life out of him.

The serpent rose up over Ob, preparing to strike.

Malvegil would not stand idle and let the gnome die. And he'd not let him be caught unawares. Not even if it brought a horde of shamblers down on them. Malvegil was about to leap up when he heard a twang.

An arrow sped out of the night and pierced the snake's neck.

The Pict! It was his arrow that struck it.

The python reeled back.

Then three things happened at once.

Ob leaped up, no trace of shock, sleep, or disorientation in his movements. He stabbed his sword through the underside of the snake's jaw. The blade went clear through and impaled its upper jaw as well.

Another arrow blasted into the snake's head.

And a single blow from Artol's sword cut the snake in two, just below its head. Where the giant warrior came from, Malvegil had no idea. One moment he was nowhere in sight, and then, he was snake slaying. Artol pounced atop the snake's body, his bulk reducing its thrashing, even as its lifeblood spilled onto the ground.

In two seconds it was over. All was still again, save for the snake's twitching, which went on for some time.

All was silent again in the camp.

The yowling and moaning of the shamblers continued unabated through it all. No hint yet that they noticed the melee with the snake.

And then from out of the guts of the dead snake, poured its young. Dozens of them, and each one near as large as a common python. They spread out in all directions. Confused. Hungry. Aggressive. They came at the men, no fear in their hearts, only hunger in their bellies.

# 15

# THE AZURE SEA, ABOARD THE MORGOVIA

*Year 801, Fourth Age*

**A**zrael the Wise clung to the schooner's rail, his knuckles white, his face pale, almost to blue; ice crusted in his black hair and clung to his boots, pants, and jacket. It made him look gray and old, though on a good day, few would mark him over forty, most would think him younger.

They'd all be wrong.

Frigid wind roared, waves pounded the ship and sent icy spray across the deck to freeze in great slabs that grew ever larger. The storm sent the boat on high, atop the waves, and then low into troughs so deep that Azrael could not see their tops. Lightning flashed over and again; all he could see by, the moons blotted out by the heavy clouds.

Bad luck was that storm. So unlucky that Azrael suspected someone acted against him with purpose — some wizard of great power, or perhaps even someone or some thing that wielded more power than any mortal sorcerer. But who? Or what? And why?

Speculation only. Always prone to paranoia was Azrael and he knew it. Those fears had grown all the worse of late, so he forced the thoughts away and concentrated on piloting the ship.

When he hired the Morgovia's captain to transport him across the Azure Sea, he negotiated a very unusual arrangement.

It was all about Azrael's cargo, you see.

Due to its sensitive nature, Azrael had to make certain that the captain and his crew were nowhere about when he loaded it aboard and secured it below deck. If they were, Azrael feared the captain would never allow that cargo on his ship.

And he wouldn't blame him.

The cargo had to remain secret — at least until they were well out at sea. The best way to ensure that was for Azrael to pilot the ship out of Tragoss Krell's docks himself, and pick up the captain and crew at the fishing village a few miles down the coast.

Suffice to say that the captain had little interest in that idea. But that changed abruptly when Azrael offered him a weighty price (nearly the full value of the ship itself) to do that, no questions asked.

Silver persuades.

Azrael piloted the ship with only his assistant, Refisal (a gnome), to aid him. Though long out of practice, Azrael was an old hand with boats, skillful enough to safely guide the schooner on his own, if only for a modest voyage in calm seas. It was harder than he anticipated, the ship larger by far than anything he'd handled without a proper crew in the past.

He moored the ship in a hidden cove several miles up the coast, to the north of Tragoss Krell.

Azrael's men and cargo were prepositioned there, awaiting the ship's arrival. The men looked haggard and worn. Almost ready to drop. Tough as they were, a few more days with the cargo and they would have broke. Most any man would. Minding that cargo was a weighty task. One that weighed on the mind even more than the body. The thick wads of wax that they stuffed in their ears helped.

Azrael and his men made certain that no prying eyes or ears were about, then they loaded the cargo and secured it in the main hold, buttoned up tight.

Azrael and Refisal set off alone in the ship. Some of the men, maybe all of them, would have stayed with him, and seen their business through to the bitter end, had Azrael but asked them. He knew that. He saw it in their eyes — the loyalty, but also the fear and the fatigue. He couldn't do that to them. They'd been through too much already. More than any man should have to bear. So he sent them on their way. A long trip home it was. Back to whatever life remained for them.

If he'd had the men sail with him to the fishing village, it would have made the voyage far easier and, more importantly, less risky with respect to the security of the cargo. But Azrael wouldn't burden his men any more. Not after all they'd been through. The fact that the short trip would be harder for him without their help was irrelevant. He took a calculated risk that no severe mishap would occur along the way that might jeopardize the cargo. A rational decision, given the short nature of the voyage and the calm seas.

With luck, Azrael figured the schooner would reach the fishing village where captain and crew awaited it within a half-day's time — assuming he didn't run it aground or somehow get lost.

Luck was absent that day.

A big storm came out of nowhere and walloped the schooner. One moment the sky was partly overcast, a pleasant, seasonable day with a light breeze, and the next moment, storm clouds appeared fully formed from parts unknown. The wind kicked up to gale force in minutes. The temperature plunged, cold and colder still. It was all Azrael could do to get the sails down before the rigging was torn to shreds. Visibility went to nothing; the sky, black as night.

The sea and storm took the *Morgovia* where it wanted — straight out to sea, which, of course, was far better than onto the rocky coast. The problem was, the frigid wind never let up. It blew for two days and two nights without respite. It carried them far from the coast. Far from civilization. Out into the depths of the trackless Azure Sea. No chance of Azrael keeping his appointment with the *Morgovia's* captain. It would be a goodly time, if ever, before the good captain saw his ship again. Through it all, Azrael was able to do little more than hang on and endure.

Azrael took solace in that they were generally headed in the right direction for their ultimate destination.

Refisal couldn't remain on deck, not with the icy spray and high winds. The old fellow wouldn't last three hours. So the duty to mind the ship fell to Azrael alone, and he accepted it stoically, though he was loath to leave Refisal alone with the cargo. He feared for the old man's safety. And for his sanity. But there was no other choice.

Where another man would have frozen to death on deck during that storm, Azrael endured. He'd never seen or heard of a storm like that on the Azure so early in the season, and never so close to the coast. Every time the waves calmed enough for him to move about, he went to battle with the ice that was everywhere — hammer, pick, and shovel in hand. He pounded on the ice to dislodge it, then shoveled it overboard. A dozen times he nearly went over the side when the ship wildly swayed, or a rogue wave slammed into it. Yet move about the deck he had to, or else the weight of the ice would swamp the vessel and send the ship and cargo to the bottom of the Azure Sea.

Perhaps that would have been for the best.

Azrael lifted the hold's hatch and peered down every couple of hours to check on the gnome and the cargo. The old man remained awake through it all. To be expected. Who could sleep through a maelstrom? Not to mention the terrible racket within the cargo hold itself. Refisal never slept much anyway. Back home, he was up at all hours tinkering with experiments in the laboratory or sitting hunched over in the library, his nose in some old tome, others stacked about him, teetering and ready to fall.

Only once during the storm did Azrael do more than lift the hold's hatch and peer in. Only once did he venture down into the hold. It was late during the first night. The cold was terrible. Ice formed on his clothes. Though he dreaded entering the hold, he needed a respite, if only for a short while. But he didn't find it there.

The howling. The screeching. The yowls, curses, and threats from the cargo were incessant and maddening. It drowned out the wind, the storm. How the old gnome endured it, Azrael had no idea. An hour was all Azrael could take of that before he fled back to the outside. He preferred the wind and the ice.

On the morning of the third day, the storm finally cleared. The moment that Refisal opened the hatch, the cursing and howling assailed Azrael's ears, no longer contained below by the thick decking. Refisal stepped up on deck looking little the worse for wear. Azrael marveled once again at the old gnome's toughness. The most reliable companion he had ever had.

"How do you stand that racket?" said Azrael.

Refisal put his hands to his ears and removed a large plug of wax from each. "When dealing with monsters, one must be prepared."

Azrael's face darkened. "They're not monsters. They're people."

"They were people, Master," said Refisal. "Good people. No longer. Now they are monsters."

# 16

# THE DEAD FENS

*Year 1242, Fourth Age
Twelfth Year of King Tenzivel's Rule*

One of swamp pythons went straight at Malvegil, its eyes affixed on him from the moment they opened. It attacked like a thing possessed, leaping through the air in a manner Malvegil thought impossible for a serpent. Malvegil batted it aside and tried to cleave it in two when it fell to the ground, but his strike missed, owing to the serpent's speed and the darkness.

Malvegil felt and heard something clang against his calf. Another snake was on him. Its jaws clamped down on his leg armor, the steel plate impenetrable (hopefully) to its jaws. Three strokes of his sword did it take to cut the thing in two; the poor angle he had, made use of the long blade difficult.

While he fought that serpent, another coiled about his other leg and began to squeeze. Its strength was uncanny. The pressure enough to cut off blood flow to his leg.

Malvegil dropped his sword and pulled his dagger. He reached down to pry the thing's head back so he could cut it off. As he did, another snake sprang through the air at his face. He turned his head at the last moment and the snake crashed fangs first into his helm with a twang.

How the helm was atop his head, he knew not. He didn't sleep with it, and didn't remember putting it on.

Finding no purchase, the snake fell and Malvegil stomped upon it, over and over, until it moved no more. By that time, his other leg was growing numb from the python that squeezed it.

And then Gorlick was there. The weapons master moved between Malvegil and the surging wave of snakes that came at them. He had a sword in one hand, a long dagger in the other, and moved like lighting — spinning, springing, crouching, and cleaving in near silence as the snakes came on. "Stay well behind me, my lord," he said quietly. Malvegil didn't need to be told twice.

Malvegil had seen Gorlick fight hundreds of times, but never like this — against snakes of all things. His mastery of the blade was a wonder to see — his crispness and precision of movement was unmatched. Even in the dark, against small, fast targets, nearly every swing of his weapons scored a hit.

For all Gorlick's skill, in the darkness, the snakes were too swift and too many for him to hold back. Some few got by him and were Malvegil's to deal with.

Malvegil had no fear of snakes, or much of anything else, so let them come, he thought. Even as he backpedaled, to stay well clear of Gorlick's blades, two more snakes struck at Malvegil's legs.

He stumbled in the dark and fell on his rump. The snakes were at him, repeatedly striking at his legs, his armor nullifying their attacks. He swiped at them, even as he grimaced from the pain in his constricted leg. He saw a momentary blur just before two more snakes slammed into his breastplate. So swift were they, he had no time to react. As one dangled from his tabard, he grabbed it about the head and squeezed. A normal man could squeeze a python all day long to little affect, but Malvegil was no common man. Strong and sturdy, muscled and thick, his power surprising even for his size.

His dagger slashed one serpent, and then it was gone, fled into the night. He smashed the head of the first snake into his armor, over and again, as it tried to coil about his arm. After several strikes the snake went limp. He dropped it, trusting it was dead or at least out of the fight. As he leaned over to deal with the two remaining snakes that still bit at his legs, he saw another spring through the air at his face.

Karktan appeared and interposed his shield at the last moment. The snake clanged into it and fell; Karktan crushed it underfoot. "Get clear," said the young warrior.

Malvegil backpedaled, thankful for the skill, bravery, and loyalty of his men. They didn't hesitate to put themselves in danger in order to defend him. What more could a Dor Lord ask for in his soldiers? They made Malvegil proud.

Malvegil swiped at the remaining snakes, their fangs clanging against his armor. But for the thick padding beneath the metal plates, those clangs would have been much the louder — and certain to have attracted the notice of the shamblers.

After a glancing blow, one snake scurried away

out of sight. The last was stubborn and kept trying to bite him even after Malvegil had cut it in half.

Malvegil's leg throbbed, one python still coiled about it, its fangs embedded into the armor at his thigh. He looked up to see Gorlick hacking with his sword this way and that, his agility, astounding, his energy, boundless.

All things considered, it was the quietest fight Malvegil had ever been in or heard tell of.

And one of the strangest.

Despite all the motion, all the killing, a man fifty paces away would not have heard a sound.

Malvegil grabbed at and stabbed the python on his leg. It was the smallest of the snakes that had attacked him, but the thing was all muscle, so powerful that when he'd sliced it near through, still it held on and squeezed him for all it was worth. Malvegil cut it in two, its blood covering his hands. He threw down its carcass in disgust and looked about.

Most of the men had gone still again, no more serpents to fight. He saw Ob smash one snake's head into a rock. Karktan stomped on another. But that was it; the battle was over.

Malvegil's plate armor had saved him. Thank the gods, he'd been cautious enough to sleep with it on. If he had been wearing common cloth, no fewer than a dozen bites would he have suffered. If the things were venomous, as he suspected they were from the way his hands stung, that would have meant his death.

Even stout Lomerian chainmail may not have offered sufficient protection from those teeth. The snakes couldn't bite through his armor plates, but they'd done their damage, his armor scraped and notched, here and there. The plate at his left calf was punctured through, though the fangs did not reach deep enough to mar his skin, or so he hoped, for he felt no pain at that spot, and no blood dripped down to his boots.

Good Lomerian armor safeguarded many of their company that night. Even so, all that saved the men from detection by the shamblers were their own steely nerves, their ability to kill swiftly and quietly, and the snakes' lack of vocalization.

After the snakes were dealt with, the men laid about the camp, weapons in hand, silent, motionless, waiting, daring to do little more than breathe and hope that the shamblers hadn't heard the skirmish. That they weren't close enough to have seen the movement. That they didn't smell the blood.

The shamblers' howls drew closer for several more minutes, and then gradually became more distant, passing by to the west of the camp. After half an hour they heard the sounds no more. The shamblers were gone. For now.

The men moved their camp about two hundred yards farther east, not easy in the night, to get well clear of the snake carcasses. They feared that other predators would smell the blood and drop by for a snack in the night. They'd have moved the snakes, but the big one was just too big. It would have taken six to ten men to move. In the bog, in the dark, it wasn't worth the risk of noise or injury. Several of the men mentioned they'd like to cook the snakes, but they all knew that they couldn't afford a fire. Not with the shamblers about.

As Malvegil settled back down to get whatever little rest he could, he was certain that he saw the Pict eating raw a big chunk he'd cut off the mother snake's carcass. Picts did such things. Civilization had not yet fully claimed them.

# 17

# THE DEAD FENS

*Year 1242, Fourth Age*
*Twelfth Year of King Tenzivel's Rule*

"It's infected," said Brother Donnelin as he examined Master Gorlick's wounded arm, Malvegil looking on. It was just before dawn, the morning after the snake attack. It was cold and the mist was heavy again about the bog.

"Can he continue?" said Malvegil as he stretched his aching muscles.

"I'm fine," said Gorlick. "It's hardly any worse than last night. Smear on some tinger leaf or brombottle and let's get moving."

"He has a mild fever," said Brother Donnelin. "With the herbs and some luck, he may be fine; the infection may pass in a day or two. But it could get worse. Maybe a lot worse. A couple of days from now we may be carrying him. I'm no Leren; there's little that I can do to treat him out here in the wild."

"That settles it," said Malvegil. "If we find nothing by midday today, we'll head back to the Dor and get Leren Tage to patch you up. Then we'll return with a larger force to scour the Fen."

Shortly before noon, they came upon a sight unexpected. A stone keep of some size with a central tower that rose a goodly height above the swamp. Once it must have been an impressive edifice – tall, stout walls adorned with carved stone cornices of intricate design and bands of bas-reliefs at every few courses of stone, ground to cornice.

But what stood before them now was as decrepit and decayed as the bog within which it resided. What little paint remained on the gray stone of the keep's walls hung in tatters and flapped in the breeze. Those sorry remnants bespoke of bygone days when bright colors and crisp pigments of azure, crimson, and mauve adorned the walls' surfaces. Tilted to one side and sunken, the lower level flooded and crumbling, the castle was much more a ruin than an abode or a fortress. Dark, dank, and barren – a fitting home for the shamblers.

Smoke billowed up from the remnants of a sizable bonfire that smoldered not far from the keep's entrance. Through the mist, which was lighter here, the men saw wisps of smoke rising here and there around the outside perimeter of the keep. It appeared that someone had lit a number of fires in scattered locations – to what purpose and end, unknown.

The men made their way slowly and carefully toward the keep, crouching low and moving from bush to bush. As they drew nearer, they heard hammering that sounded like carpenters working. When they reached to within 150 yards of the walls, they dropped down on their bellies and crawled. Soon, they saw figures moving around by the keep's entrance. Workmen, doing something, though the distance was still too great to tell who they were or what exactly they were doing.

Here the mist was welcome, for without it, given the sparse and low vegetation, the men surely would have been spotted by the workers had they but looked in their direction.

Gabriel sniffed the air and looked to Red Tybor who nodded knowingly in return.

"What?" said Malvegil having noticed their exchange. "What do you sense?"

Ob inhaled deeply and then paused a moment. "Stinking Lugron," he said. "Well, at least we know how to deal with them."

"That can't be right; they can't be Lugron," said Malvegil. He sniffed the air. "I don't smell anything other than this putrid swamp. Besides, there have never been Lugron in these lands. Not on my borders. And not this far south."

"I'm afraid that now there are," said Gabriel.

About one hundred yards from the castle, a shallow, muddy ditch cut through the bog parallel to the castle's wall, bushes lining its rim, a trickle of a stream within it. Despite the wet, it was the perfect spot to remain out of sight and watch. The men slithered into the ditch, scrambled across, and drew up on the far side, their eyes peeking between the bushes.

"I care not for the look of this place," whispered Malvegil.

"What did you expect, lordling," said Ob playfully, "a pristine tower of white, and a fairy princess beckoning you hither with promises of rewards and favors for her rescue?"

Uncharacteristically, Malvegil shrugged off the

remark.

"I've never faced the Lugron in battle, but I've heard many stories about them," said Karktan as they settled into the ditch, choosing the driest spots they could find. "Most say they're more monster than man, and that they're dumber than rocks. Some hint that they're more than that. Where lies the truth?"

"In the eyes of the beholder, as always," said Master Gorlick.

"They're stupid brutes," said Malvegil. "Not much better than animals. Kill them as you find them, as you would a wild boar or a rogue bear."

"They are men," said Gabriel. "Not too unlike you or I. As much a race of men as are the Volsung, Picts, Elves, Gnomes, Dwarves, and Smallfolk. Think less of them only at your own peril."

"The Lugron are an old race," said Red Tybor. "Older even than my people. In ancient times, there were many more of them that roamed about Midgaard, in bands large and small. Now there are fewer. Now they stay to the northern lands, the mountains, mostly. Through all the years, they've been the mortal enemies of the other races, for they see all who are not of their own kind as quarry to be hunted on sight. Sometimes for sport. Sometimes for spoils. Sometimes for food."

"So it's true that they are cannibals?" said Karktan.

"Some Lugron have done such things," said Gabriel.

"More than some," said Aradon. "I've seen their handiwork any number of times."

"They particularly enjoy gnomes," said Red Tybor, at which Ob shot him an ugly glance. "When the winters run long, and the snow covers the ground for many months, the Lugron go hunting for men."

"Desperate men do desperate things, Lugron or not," said Gabriel. "Make no mistake, though men they be, they are our enemies. Lugron seek our deaths so that they can rule all the lands, hunt freely, and roam where they will. Individually they are not evil at heart though many are cruel and do evil deeds – it is in their culture to do so, not their nature, I think."

"You're too generous, Gabe," said Ob. "They're here and that means we're to kill them or they us. That's the way of things. Always has been; always will be, until one side is wiped out. That's when there will be peace between us. And only then. Since there ain't that many of them bastards left in the North, it's them what's gonna be wiped out, not us. And good riddance to them."

Gabriel looked down; a sad expression on his face. "The mountains yet harbor many of their kind. They remain a threat; a grave one."

# 18

# THE DEAD FENS, OUTSIDE THE KEEP

*Year 1242, Fourth Age
Twelfth Year of King Tenzivel's Rule*

Red Tybor slithered close to Malvegil. "The bonfires. I would know what they're about."

The bonfire closest to them was the largest, a dozen feet across at least. It still spouted a bit of flame and a mass of hot embers, but mostly it gave off gray smoke. A long plume of it trailed off into the overcast sky. The other fires farther afield were smaller; no flames remained, though wisps of smoke still rose from each. "Can you get close enough without being seen?" said Malvegil.

"If the mist and my luck holds," said Red Tybor.

"Do it."

Red Tybor was about halfway to the nearest bonfire when he dropped down flat. He turned and signaled to the men back in the ditch to go down and quiet.

And they did.

Moments later, they caught a whiff of the shamblers' stench, though none of them were in sight. It was a smell akin to rotten meat, but much stronger; more intense even than the stink of a skunk or a gronsel. It preceded the shamblers, and overwhelmed the decaying miasma of the putrid bog.

Soon, the Lugron smelled the shamblers too. In a near panic, they scrambled inside the keep's only visible entrance, a large wooden door that sagged on one hinge but only blocked half the opening; its companion door rested against the stone wall several feet from where it belonged. Both doors were battered and scarred. They had planks nailed across them, as if repaired in haste.

After the Lugron fled beyond the doorway, they dropped an iron portcullis that barred further ingress to the keep. It jammed halfway down. They struggled with it. Several Lugron pulled and heaved on the bars until it finally lowered into place.

Soon came the now familiar croaking of the shamblers. Then the moaning. This time, the sounds were intermittent and much weaker than those the men had heard during the night. As if the light of the day, as limited as it was, drained the energy from the creatures. As if they were half-asleep. Groggy or not, the things were close. Very close. Hidden from view only by the mist.

The suspense was maddening to the men as they lay in that ditch. It seemed the sounds were coming from the east, off to their right. But by the sound of it, the shamblers were spread out. Some might walk out of the mist close to the ditch, or even behind it. The men had no cover. Nowhere to hide. They tightly gripped their weapons and readied themselves to spring into action if they were seen.

At last, from out of the murk, came a nightmare. A shambling horde of lumbering death.

# 19

# THE AZURE SEA, ABOARD THE MORGOVIA

*Year 801, Fourth Age*

"Three weeks, Master," said Refisal as he sat beside Azrael on the *Morgovia*'s deck, the boat rocking up and down as the ship made its way south, a moderate wind helping it along its way. "You still haven't told me where we're going."

"Ten times I've told you," said Azrael. "An island."

"But you haven't said which one."

"What difference does it make?"

"The inhabitants won't like our cargo."

"It's uninhabited."

Refisal sighed with relief. "I was hoping you'd say that, Master." He unfurled a navigational chart.

"It's not on there," said Azrael. "It's not on any chart that I've ever seen, and for good reason. Few who venture there or thereabouts ever return."

The gnome's eyebrows went up. "What danger lurks there?"

"A beast," said Azrael. "A sea creature left over from ancient days. From the Age of Myth and Legend."

"What good does that do us?" said Refisal.

"Would you have the beast kill them, rather than us?"

"The beast allows entry to the island. Usually. But it permits no one to leave."

"So it will contain them?" said Refisal.

"Forevermore."

"That seems a perfect solution to our dilemma," said Refisal, "except that we'll be stuck there too. With them."

"This is possible," said Azrael. "But I've escaped there before. I believe I can do so again."

"By the gods, I hope so," said the gnome. "I cannot stand being near these things much longer. The stench is quite—"

Azrael laughed. "Don't worry, old friend. I can outwit the beast. We will sight the island soon, drop them off, and soon thereafter, we'll take the homeward road. Once we've found the cure, we'll return again, and restore them to their former selves."

"Do you truly believe that we'll be successful?" said Refisal. "That we'll find the cure?"

"I have to believe it," said Azrael. "I have to."

## 20

# THE DEAD FENS, OUTSIDE THE KEEP

*Year 1242, Fourth Age
Twelfth Year of King Tenzivel's Rule*

Despite the haze, and some little distance, the light of day afforded the men a far better look at the shamblers than they had during the battle at the longboat. They were truly wretched, horrid monstrosities. Their flesh, decayed; their skin, mottled and loose, though not bloated like those they fought before. Most exhibited terrible wounds: an eye missing here, an ear there, an arm gone, a leg missing, chunks of flesh torn away. Those pitiful creatures were no victims of any wasting disease, nor were they deformed or injured men. That much was now abundantly clear. No further debate was needed.

It was clear because some of them walked even though their rib cages were splayed open, their organs exposed. Nearly all of the shamblers limped and staggered, some dragging entrails that hung from gaping abdominal wounds. A bizarre, surreal sight it was, almost comical in its weirdness, if not for the fact that it was real, and that the creatures were as deadly as they were horrific.

To Malvegil's eyes, some of the shamblers

looked gnawed upon. As if they had had bites torn out of their flesh. As if they had been partially eaten. One creature's head dangled limply from its neck, which was clearly broken. And yet it still walked, and did so as well as any of its companions.

Those shamblers may have been living men once, but no longer. Now their very existence was a blasphemy against all that is holy and right in the world. For now, they were the walking dead; animated corpses risen from some cursed grave by forbidden, unnatural forces. The antithesis of life were they. And yet, in some strange sense they were not dead at all, for they did walk. They did hunger. They did yearn, if but only for blood, flesh, and souls.

Undead.

That is what they were. A mockery of life.

Undead.

That olden term pulled from prehistory perhaps described them best. A strange, archaic word, it was. It lingered only in ancient song, rhyme, faerie tales, and ghost stories. What fell magic, dark arts, or outré madness imbued that misshapen spark of life on those piteous creatures? None amongst the group could say. Not one dared to guess.

Several dozen of the undead there were – spread out across a wide expanse of the bog. All moving generally westward, such that they'd pass between the keep and Malvegil's group. Some would pass very close to the ditch.

Too close.

Surprisingly, the creatures moved more

quietly through the bog than had the men. Why that was, Malvegil could only guess. Perhaps because they were not weighed down with armor and gear, no metal to clank on metal, and less weight to sink their feet into the loam. Or perhaps it was something more — some strange side effect of whatever wickedness gave them a semblance of life and locomotion. Whatever the answer, on they came.

## 21

# THE DEAD FENS, OUTSIDE THE KEEP

*Year 1242, Fourth Age
Twelfth Year of King Tenzivel's Rule*

The mist limited vision to thirty yards at best, much less in some directions, but there was nowhere for Red Tybor to take cover. Nowhere to hide from the dead.

Red Tybor nocked an arrow but held it. He looked back to Malvegil for some sign or signal. Alone as he was, too far out for any to give him aid, there was still no fear in his eyes. That man feared nothing.

"Make no move. Wait for my command," whispered Malvegil to those near him. He signaled the same to Red Tybor.

Some few at the undead's van passed close to the keep, some almost at the walls, though they paid it no heed, neither stopping or pausing nor approaching the gate, staring only straight ahead or down at the ground as they went.

One creature shambled out of the haze not twenty feet from where Red Tybor lay, its jaw hanging limp, dislocated; its cheek, torn open; blackened teeth kissing the air. It looked directly at the Pict, or seemed to, but continued on its way, as if Red Tybor were not there at all. Other shamblers passed just as close to the ditch, one nearly stumbled in. None of them paid Red Tybor any heed.

And the men made no move against them.

That was hard for them to do: to stay still, to hold back. So much easier it would have been to charge into action. To fight. To do what they were trained to do. What they did best. But they were no fools. Every man amongst them knew that even if they overcame the dead, the Lugron would lock the keep up tight against them. They'd suffer badly to get in, if ever they could. To complete their mission, they had to stay unseen. Keep their presence unknown. So against all their instincts, they remained still. Still as statues. Silent as stone.

And the dead made no move against them. It was as if the men didn't exist. Perhaps the things were blind. Perhaps they hunted by sound or scent or some strange unnatural sense unknown to the living.

As the undead horde shambled along, suddenly, a hare sprang from a hole and bounded off. The nearest of the dead leaped into action, croaking as they sped after the rabbit. Their shambling, meandering gait gone. Now they jumped and sprinted with as much speed and agility as any living man. The other dead caught sight of either the hare or their fellows, and within several moments, the entire mob was flying after the unlucky rabbit.

Fully half the croaking, gibbering horde sped past between Red Tybor and the men in the ditch, oblivious of their presence. The men remained still and quiet until the dead were out of sight and for a goodly while thereafter. Only then did they dare breathe. Only then did they loosen their grips on their weapons, their knuckles stiff, their hands pained.

"Unless they're blind, they could not have failed to see us," said McDuff.

"It's motion that attracts them," said Malvegil. "Though some looked directly at us, they didn't seem to see us, but as soon as that rabbit moved, they were on him."

"They also react to sound," said Gabriel. "They cocked their heads to the side, listening as their fellows made their noises."

"So if we're still and quiet the buggers will pass us by?" said McDuff.

"They just did," said Gabriel.

"But will it work again?" said McDuff. "I'd prefer a straight up fight, myself."

"Do we follow them?" asked Brother Donnelin.

They all looked to Gabriel who was fidgeting around with his ankh.

"What is that thing anyways?" asked Malvegil. "What is it really?"

"Just a tool from olden days," said Gabriel.

"And you claim it has a power to it?" said Malvegil. "A magic?"

"It does."

"But are you certain that it still works?" said Malvegil. "The darned thing's got more scars than the bar in Baylock's Rest."

"It led us here, did it not?" said Gabriel. "It will serve."

"Well I don't think your thingamabob is set

right," said Ob. "The stinking Lugron hid from the shamblers, same as us. It seems, they've got nothing to do with them. The morons can't even fix the stinking gate properly. Maybe we're in the wrong place. Maybe we should be following them things," he said, pointing after the dead.

"Aye," said Red Tybor. "The gnome is right. We should follow them. Kill them all and be done with this. Those things must be put down."

"And they will be," said Gabriel. "But right now, this keep is where we need to be."

"We came here to rescue people that were kidnapped," said Malvegil. "The shamblers didn't kidnap anyone. It was the Lugron. They're the ones we're after. We can come back later with a larger force to deal with the dead."

"You're speculating, the both of you," said Ob. "We don't even know that anyone got kidnapped. Them dead things may have killed everyone on the boat and dragged off the bodies. The Lugron may have nothing to do with it."

"The shamblers wore seamen's garb," said Gabriel. "At least half of them, as best I could tell."

"What?" said Malvegil.

"Looked like rags to me," said Aradon. "All hanging in tatters."

"Gabe's right," said Ob. "Now that I think about, those tattered rags did look like the remnants of seamen's uniforms. The colors were right; the cut of the shirts."

"You're not saying that those things are the seamen from the boats that went missing, are you?" said Malvegil.

"He is," said Ob. "And I'd bet money he's right.

Ten silver stars, if anyone is up for it."

"How?" said Malvegil. "What could have happened to make them like that?"

"Some kind of disease, it must be," said Ob.

"Chaos sorcery," said Par Talbon, his voice deadly serious. "I've sensed it throughout the Fens, and it's stronger here. Black magic of some olden style I've not felt afore."

"I agree," said Brother Donnelin. "The dark powers are at work here. "The hand of Helheim has left its mark upon this place."

"Hand of Helheim, my ass," said Ob. "Superstitious bunk."

"A fiend did this," said Gabriel. His words caught the attention of all the men. "Someone with no respect for the sanctity of life, for dignity, for all that is natural and holy in the world. We may already be too late to rescue anyone. They may all be as those lost souls," he said as he gestured toward where the undead had gone.

"What purpose would it serve to do that to a man?" said Aradon. "To make him into such a creature?"

"Who knows the mind of a fiend?" said Gabriel. "Mayhap it's experimenting on them for its own pleasure or some dark purpose that we cannot guess. Maybe it's using them as guards, or foot soldiers. Who knows."

"Or, like I said," countered Ob, "it might just be some stinking disease what's done this to them. A weird one, no doubt, but just a disease; a plague of some sort. Like leprosy or wasting sickness. Gabe — you mentioned that yourself a while back."

"I was wrong," said Gabriel. "It's no natural disease."

Ob looked shocked. "Well that's a first," he said. "Gabriel Garn admits that he's wrong about something. A historic day this is—"

"Ob," said Aradon sternly.

"Somebody doesn't have to be behind this," said Ob. "And we need not invoke any devils of myth and legend to explain it either. These are not olden days, they are modern times. We are civilized men. Educated. Worldly. We must think with our brains, not with our superstitions."

"Whatever or whoever is behind this," said Malvegil. "We must put a stop to it. Man, monster, or disease, it doesn't matter to me. That's why we're here. We're going to go in there and rout out whatever Lugron are hold up in the place, and anyone else what's in there with them. Then we'll get whatever truth there is to get out of them. One way or another, we will get to the bottom of this."

"And if I'm right, and it's a disease?" said Ob. "Going in there, up close and personal with them stinking Lugron, we could catch it. Do you want to end up like them shamblers? Your flesh falling off, your guts hanging out?"

"We've already been exposed," said Gabriel. "Up close and personal during the fight at the longboat. Fleeing now will do us little good, and it may bring others harm."

"Gabe's right," said Aradon. "If it is a disease, the longer we stay away from everyone else, the better. We don't want to spread it through the countryside, or to the folks at Dor Malvegil and beyond. Once we're through here and we know we don't have it, we head home. A week or so and we'll know, one way or the other."

"Master Gorlick can't wait a week," said Donnelin. "He can't wait even two days. We need to get his arm seen to properly, and soon. If the infection worsens, he could be dead in a week."

"It's nothing," said Gorlick. "I'll be fine."

"We'll have supplies brought over from the longship," said Malvegil. "Or I'll have someone fetch Leren Tage to us."

"And if there's nothing to find inside?" said Ob. "Just a stinking Lugron den?"

"Then we'll follow the trail of the shamblers, as Red Tybor suggested," said Malvegil. "We'll hunt them. We'll kill them. And we'll be done with this."

## 22

# THE HOLLOW, AZRAEL'S MANOR

*Year 801, Fourth Age*

**R**efisal barged through the laboratory's door exhibiting more energy and emotion than was common for the old gnome. "Master, do you hear it, the yelling?"

Azrael looked up, a bubbling test tube in one hand, a decanter of swirling green liquid in the other, odd, chemical odors in the air, as was usual for the place. Mice scurried about in small cages atop the table in front of Azrael, tiny bowls of liquid within, one blue, one red, one clear, the fourth empty. "What say you?"

"A girl downstairs, terribly ill, perhaps dying," said Refisal. "Her mother brought her, and begs for help."

"They brought her here, to my manor?" said Azrael. "Could it be a ruse to gain entry? Are they armed?"

"The little girl seems quite ill, Master."

"Send her to the herbalist at once. He may have some potion. Send two men with them to help; horses if they need them. Have they coin for the herbalist?"

"They've been there," said Refisal as his eyes studied the latest experiments that lay before his master. "He could do nothing for her. Or rather, nothing he tried worked. Mother Aulran couldn't help either. Have you had a breakthrough?"

"The mice are responding better than we hoped," said Azrael. "There's no sign of illness in the blue group. The red also shows improvement; they're sick, but all still alive. Half the control group is dead, the rest soon to join them. I was just about to try another variation that may improve even on the blue. We're on to something with these formulations. I think we're close this time. Very close."

The gnome nodded and looked happy in his way, which is to say, he wasn't expressionless and wore no scowl. "The girl's mother says you're her only hope."

"I'm an alchemist, not a Leren," said Azrael. "Tell her that."

"You're a wizard, Master," said Refisal. "And you're not fooling anyone by denying it. That's why they're here. I've seen you do wonders that'd be the envy of any Tower Wizard. Others have too. Surely, you can do something for her? You will try at least?"

"I only dabble in magic. Science is my realm, as you should well know. They are not one and the same."

"If you say so, Master."

Azrael put down his instruments and closed his writing journal. "I will do what I can," said Azrael. He loaded up a bag with various jars and capsules, powders and herbs, unguents and strange instruments of metal, and then the two made their way to the staircase.

Marple, the House Butler, met them near the top of the stairs. He looked anxious and flustered. He opened his mouth to speak, but a wave of Azrael's hand cut him off.

"I've been informed," said Azrael. "Rouse a squad of guardsmen, just in case."

"Of course, Master," said Marple, a confused look on his face. "In case of what?"

"In case they're thieves or worse," said Azrael.

"Of course, Master."

The stair's wide, curved arc gave Azrael a goodly view of his guests in the front parlor (and they of him) well before he stood before them.

The girl lay on the couch, moaning. Her face was sickly white, tinged of blue, her breathing shallow, her eyes closed. A pretty thing she was. Blonde hair, thin, and well formed of face and limb. A child of six, seven at the most. Her mother, an unusually attractive woman in her mid-thirties, of long red hair and green eyes. Well dressed. She wore a bejeweled headband across her forehead — a noblewoman of high station.

"Are you Azrael, the wizard?" said the mother at first sight, shouting up to him as he descended the marble steps. She wrung her hands with worry.

He didn't respond until he stood directly before her. "I am Azrael," he said, "but I'm an alchemist, not a wizard."

She looked on the verge of panic. "They said you were a wizard. They said you could help. They said it."

"I will help if I can, but I'm no healer," said Azrael. "And I'm certainly no Leren."

She calmed a bit and took a breath. No doubt she feared being turned out into the night. "I'm Lady Cassandra of Farthing Heights," said the woman. "My daughter, Pennebray. You're our last hope. The herbalist gave her three different potions. They dulled the pain for a time, but it came back all the fiercer. Mother Aulran could do no better. The townsfolk say that you can work wonders. And a wonder is what we need."

"What troubles your daughter?"

"Pains in her head," she said, her voice quaking. "So bad that she vomits. She can't keep anything down. Not even water. So dizzy is she that she can barely walk even when the pain subsides. It came on of a sudden in the middle of the night a ten day ago."

"How is her breathing?"

"Unencumbered."

"Did she fall? Hit her head?"

"We found no bump, no cut, nothing."

"The day she fell ill, and the day before, did she eat any strange food? Anything the rest of you didn't try?"

"Nothing. She and I ate the same."

"No berries picked in the woods?"

"Goldenberries, perhaps. We eat them all the time. But she knows them well. And she knows what berries to avoid."

Azrael carefully and slowly felt all around the girl's head. Then he checked her breathing, felt and counted her pulse at wrist and at neck. He checked her reflexes, looked into her mouth, eyes, and ears using curious instruments of his own design. When he was done, he stood tall, and stared down at the girl, holding her small hand in his, a concerned expression on his face, his eyes blinking and glistening.

"What is it?" said Lady Cassandra. "What afflicts her? Is it a poison? A curse?"

"Why speak you of curses and poisons?" said Azrael.

"The Widow Lothborg has always been jealous. I think she's a witch and I'm not afraid to say it. I see her staring at my baby, hatred on her face. She has no children of her own. A bitter, bitter old hag. She's no good. No good at all, that woman."

"Was your daughter in contact with her before she became sick? Eaten any food in her presence or that she may have prepared?"

"I keep her well away from that witch, always. But that wouldn't stop her from casting a spell from afar. Not that I know of such things, but that woman can't be trusted. I wouldn't put it past her to hurt an innocent child. Why does she hate me so? What did I ever do to her? It's not my fault she's an ugly, frumpy old hag. She's—"

"I believe your daughter suffers from a swelling of the brain," said Azrael. "Though from what cause, I cannot say, except to say it is surely not a curse. Expel thoughts of the preternatural from your mind. They will do neither you nor your daughter any service. There is a tea that I can prepare that may help. It may lessen the symptoms for a time, but it will not cure her. Such ailments often go away by themselves, given time for the swelling to subside."

"Will it? It's been ten days already, and she

grows worse each day."

"I don't know."

"My baby is going to die, isn't she? That's what you mean, but you fear to say it. Tell me that I am wrong. I am not a weak woman. I would have the truth."

"Her fate is in the hands of the gods, my Lady. But the tea may help. I can also make a potion that will dull her pain, something perhaps more potent than what the herbalist gave her. I know of nothing more to do than that."

The girl was able to keep down the tea, and within half an hour, she drifted off to a peaceful sleep. Almost immediately, her mother passed out next to her.

"What truly ails the girl, Master?" said Refisal.

"Just as I said, a swelling in the head, or so, I believe. But whether it's her brain swelling due to some infection, or a growth within causing the pressure, I cannot say. I gave her the strongest dose of the anti-inflammatory that I dare. The same for the pain reducer. Even so, she'll have relief for no more than six or eight hours."

"And then?"

"Then we give her more. And then again every six hours until the symptoms subside or death claims her. I wish I could do more, but I cannot."

"What of your latest serum? Could it cure her?"

"If only it were so," said Azrael. "There is much animal testing that yet needs to be done before I can inject a person with it. If only our experiments were a few months farther along, we might well be able to save her. But as things stand now, we cannot. Her fate lies in the hands of the gods."

# 23

# THE DEAD FENS, OUTSIDE THE KEEP

*Year 1242, Fourth Age
Twelfth Year of King Tenzivel's Rule*

Gabriel fingered the ankh that hung from his neck, twirling it slowly on its cord. "What we seek is within those walls," he said. "Inside that keep. Of that, I'm certain."

"How do you know that?" said Ob, his eyes drifting to the ankh.

"He knows things," said Aradon. "Just accept it."

"That's crap," said Malvegil. "Ob is right. Nothing but bunk and bother." Malvegil turned toward Brother Donnelin. "Priest, what do your rune stones say?"

"Oh, boy, here we go," muttered Ob as he shook his head. "Throw down the bones, Donnelin! Let the stinking rocks tell us what to do. That's always smart. The rocks know everything, don't they?" he said shaking his head in frustration.

Donnelin looked to Aradon who nodded his permission. The priest shook the leather bag that hung from his belt, and dumped a collection of rune stones on a flat area of ground. Most of the stones were granite. Some few were marble.

Nearly all were polished to a shine on all sides, their surfaces smooth and hard. Most were rectangular. Others were round or oval, or irregularly shaped, but all were of a size to easily fit three or four within the palm of a hand. Despite their hardness, they were chipped at their edges and scratched here and there about their surfaces from long years of frequent use. All had runic glyphs of red or white pigment inscribed in them. Each glyph had its meaning, though few beyond the priests could read them, and fewer still could interpret their message when "the bones were thrown," as they say.

Brother Donnelin sat cross-legged and intently studied the stones for some moments, looking from one to another, to another, as was his custom.

Then he gasped: a harsh, sharp sound that caught in his throat.

His face went expressionless. He grew unnaturally pale. Sweat beaded on his brow. Never before had he behaved thus when reading the stones.

He rocked back and forth, back and forth.

His eyes rolled back in his head — a frightful sight that made the men gasp.

"Donnelin?" said Aradon, but the priest did not react to his voice. "Donnelin," he shouted.

"Quietly," said Gabriel, steel in his voice.

Ob put a hand to the priest's shoulder and shook him gently, then harder when he failed to respond. "Donnelin, you stinking slacker. Snap out of it. What's come over you? Are you all right?"

The priest still didn't respond; Ob's face grew

concerned, his voice, strained. "Get me some water to dump on him."

Gabriel moved to Donnelin's side. He studied him for a moment, then lifted up his ankh and carefully pressed it against the cleric's forehead.

Donnelin immediately slumped forward and gulped for air, breathing heavily, as if he had been holding his breath. Sweat poured down his brow. He turned this way and that; his eyes filled with terror. His whole body shook.

"Be calm," said Gabriel. "You are safe, my friend. We are with you."

Donnelin nodded his understanding but was unable to speak. His mouth moved, but the words would not pass his lips. He took a cup of water offered to him and drank deeply. His breathing soon returned to normal.

"What did you see?" asked Gabriel. "Tell us true."

"A nightmare," said Donnelin shaking his head. "I don't understand it. I don't want to think of it. I can't."

"You must," said Gabriel. "Tell us quickly."

"Spit it out, man," said Malvegil.

"Don't pressure him," said Ob. "He's ill. Give him a moment."

"I was looking at the bones, trying to get a reading," said Donnelin, his eyes wide, his voice strained, "same as I've done a thousand times. But of a sudden, strange images appeared in my mind's eye. Things I've never seen afore; places I've never been. Then thoughts that were not my own flooded into my head."

"I tried to hold them back, but I could not.

They were too strong. Relentless. They crashed through my mind, trampling my will as if it were nothing. As if I were nothing.

"Bizarre thoughts; crazed; the ramblings of a madman. They mesmerized me, rooting me in place. I could not move, nor call out, nor free myself of their yoke. No matter how much I struggled, I could do nothing.

"I didn't know where I was. For a moment, I didn't know who I was. I couldn't remember anything." Donnelin lowered his head and cradled his brow in his hands."

"Do not fear," said Gabriel. "You are free of it now. But you must tell us the rest. There is more, I think."

Donnelin looked up, his eyes watery; anguish on his face. He spoke softly, his voice but a whisper. "This be an evil place. The air, the ground, the smells, everything about it; evil. You were right, Sir Gabriel. Its master is an ancient fiend from a bygone age – from a time so alien, so ancient, it's unimaginable. Though I fathom not its nature, and cannot name it or describe it, I know, just as surely as I know anything, that there, within the stone walls of that keep, dwells a madness that could swallow the world. A plague that could bring an end to all life on Midgaard. An end to all we hold dear. I can say no more than that, and that much fades even now from my mind, thank the gods."

The men exchanged worried glances.

"We came out here for pirates," said Ob. "Do any of you dimwits even remember that?"

"Why can't it be stinking pirates?" Ob said.

"For anyone else, pirates would be bad news, but for us, no. For us, pirates are too darn easy."

"And boring.

"We need more excitement than that, don't we, my boys?

"For us, it's got to be a big baddie.

"And the whole stinking world has got to be in jeopardy too — on the verge of ending, doesn't it?

"Can't just be pirates," said Ob. "No, sir. We need a fiend out the past."

"A fiend!

"Hey, why not Loki himself? And maybe a dragon or two along with him, just to make things more interesting?

"And why not go and call up Azathoth or Bhaal while we're at it? Summon them right up out of Helheim.

"Madness.

"Madmen.

"And fools.

"I'm surrounded by them." The gnome shook his head and sat down.

"Did the fiend sense you?" said Gabriel to Donnelin. "Think carefully before you answer. Did he notice your presence? Did he acknowledge you in any way?"

Donnelin shook his head. "The thoughts were so chaotic, I cannot say for certain, but as far as I know, he did not think of me, did not react to me. And he never cast his gaze upon me, thank Odin. For if he had, my sanity, whatever little is left of it, surely would have fled."

Malvegil shook his head and moved away from the priest. "It's already fled," he muttered. "The gnome is right. Ancient fiends, my ass. Superstitious drivel."

# 24

# THE DEAD FENS, OUTSIDE THE KEEP

*Year 1242, Fourth Age
Twelfth Year of King Tenzivel's Rule*

McDuff pulled a metal flask from beneath his jerkin. He unscrewed the stopper and offered the flask to Donnelin. "Have some of this, laddie. It will perk you up a bit, I promise."

Ob snatched the flask from McDuff's hand and took a long swill. "Decent stuff. You should try it." He passed it to Donnelin.

"What is it?" said the priest.

"Dwarven rum," said McDuff. "A little recipe I acquired from the best spirit maker in all of Darendon. It will put hairs on your chest and thicken your beard up too. Only a sip now; it has quite a kick to it."

Donnelin sniffed it. He wrinkled his nose and blinked several times as if it stung his eyes.

"Just a sip, laddie," said McDuff. "Go on now. It will do you good."

Donnelin swallowed a mouthful. His cheeks went red and his face contorted in a look of disgust. He chased the rum down with a long drink of water from his canteen. "Horrid. My throat is on fire. Are you trying to kill me?"

McDuff looked disappointed. "You've no

appreciation of good spirits, priest. But have another sip anyway. It'll do you good whether you care for the taste or not."

Donnelin did and cringed again, his face all scrunched up like a prune. "Tasted a lot better the second time, since the first numbed my mouth, tooth to tonsil."

Gorlick groaned and clutched at his arm. He was down at the end of the line of men, farthest from the leaders, but they heard his cry.

"I need to check him," said Donnelin.

"You're in no shape for that," said McDuff. "We're still checking you."

"There's no one else," said Donnelin. "Help me up."

"Take it slow," said Aradon. Donnelin took a deep breath and one last mouthful of McDuff's rum, then crawled over to Gorlick, Artol aiding him along the way.

"Is the pain worse?" said Donnelin to Gorlick.

Gorlick nodded, his jaw set. He was not a man who complained.

The cleric undid Gorlick's bandages.

"**Y**our priest has cracked," whispered Malvegil to Aradon. "Visions in his head? Hogwash and horsefeathers. The man has lost it. The stress has gotten to him. You should have chosen a more seasoned House Cleric. He's too young. Too flighty."

"He's always been level headed," said Aradon, "but what he just told us makes little sense to me."

"What he saw frightened him out of his wits,"

said Gabriel. "When that happens, the mind plays tricks. How much of what he said is truth, how much is fancy, we won't know until we get in there."

Donnelin gasped at the sight of Gorlick's arm.

"What?" said Gorlick in a panic. "How bad? Let me see."

The others all turned to look.

"The wound festers badly," said Donnelin. "It's much worse than it was this morning. We'll need to get you straight back to Dor Malvegil after this, plague or no. Lean back now and I'll clean the wound as best I can and rebind it."

Gorlick pulled his arm free from the priest's grip and stared at the wound for several moments, then tightly closed his eyes and looked away. He'd seen many wounds in his time. He knew what it meant. Even if he survived it, he would lose his arm. They'd have to cut it off to end the infection and burn his flesh at the stump to keep him from bleeding to death. He'd seen it done many times. He'd never be the same after that. He'd never be whole again. He'd never wield a second weapon. He'd never be the finest swordsman in all Lomion again. Never again.

"Yesterday that wound was minor," said Malvegil. "The priest cleaned it good and proper, dressed it with a poultice, and bandaged it as good as any Leren could. And now, one day later, he looks half dead. By the look of it, his arm is lost. What could do that? In one day? A poison? Some venom in the bite of those things, do you think?"

"I don't know," said Aradon. "This is outside my experience. It should not have gotten so bad, so quickly, if ever."

"Not a poison," said Gabriel. "Something else, though I fathom not its nature. It's something more insidious."

"Death," whispered Red Tybor who had crawled up beside them. "There is naught but death here. I fear we will not leave this place, just as those others did not."

"What others?" said Malvegil.

"The bonfire was full of bodies," said Red Tybor. "The Lugron burned them. They at least think it's a plague."

That remark gave the men pause, for Red Tybor normally brimmed with confidence.

"What could be in there?" said Aradon as he looked toward the castle. "Could it truly be a fiend, a thing out of Helheim?"

"I sense an ancient power here," said Gabriel. "It lurks within the keep, just as Donnelin said. I'm not certain what it is. Mayhap it is a demon from the old world. Something left over from the Age of Myth and Legend. Something whose origins are not of this world. But from wherever it hails, now it is the master of the Fens; the master of the dead, and the key to their destruction."

Malvegil's brows went up. He looked at Gabriel as if he were a madman.

"I know how that sounds," said Gabriel. "But such things have happened afore. The dark corners of the world yet harbor ancient mysteries, monsters, creatures of legend. Normal folk never see such things. Even men like us don't see them every day, but that doesn't make them myth. It doesn't make them fairy stories."

"We're but days away from the largest city in the civilized world," said Malvegil. "Not some dark corner of anything."

"We might as well be," said Gabriel. "Hardly anyone comes to the Fens. And most of those that do, don't ever return home. Maybe what's in that keep is why. This may have been going on for a long time, right under our noses. Just look at that place," he said, gesturing toward the keep. "It's old. Ancient. Who knows how long the fiend has dwelled within. All this time, we thought it was the swamp that took people. Mayhap it was Donnelin's fiend."

Malvegil huffed and shook his head. "I fear the gnome is right. You're all madmen. When you speak your minds, your insanity spills out. Helheim is not even a real place. It's just a myth from the old stories. Legends and tall tales. There's little truth to them."

"Helheim is a real place," said Gabriel. "As is Nifleheim. As real as Midgaard."

"How would you know?" said Malvegil.

"I know," said Gabriel.

"Hogwash," said Malvegil.

"If it's a real place," said Malvegil. "How does one get there? Which direction is it? What road do you take? How far?"

"It's more complicated than that," said Gabriel.

"It's bullshit, is what it is," said Malvegil.

"I know little of demons," said Aradon. "I am a man of fact and fist, not superstition and old religions. But whatever it is that's in there, if it is behind the shamblers and the takings of those ships, I will see it dead, whatever it is: man, fiend, Lugron, or whatnot."

"That much I agree with," said Malvegil. "So let's have at the Lugron without further delay, and push through to their master, if they truly have one. If he turns over captives unharmed, I may be inclined to let him live. Otherwise, I'll hang his head from his own walls."

"There could be many more Lugron inside," said Red Tybor. "We could find ourselves roasted over a spit, apples in our mouths—"

"Or hanging from the walls," said Ob.

"We'll deal with the Lugron," said Malvegil. "Regardless of how many there are. They are enemies that we know well how to fight."

# 25

# THE HOLLOW, AZRAEL'S MANOR

*Year 801, Fourth Age*

Not two hours after taking the tea, the girl awoke screaming. She cupped her hands against the sides of her head. She was in agony, the pain incessant. So bad, she could not speak coherently.

"Do something," shouted Lady Cassandra as Azrael raced down the stair. "Please, give her something, anything. Anything that will take the pain away."

"She's my baby. Please. She doesn't deserve this. She's done nothing wrong.

"Nothing!"

Azrael looked into Lady Cassandra's eyes. Such pain. Such fear. Dread. And pleading. Begging. Azrael wanted so badly to help her daughter. To save the poor child. An innocent little life. Azrael felt his throat constrict, his heart raced. He felt moisture at his eyes.

All that shocked him.

His reaction shocked him.

Not many things moved Azrael to emotion. True, strong emotion. He'd seen too much for too long. His heart was hardened to such things. Even terrible things. But he felt for these people. For the child. But at the same time, he resented being under that pressure. Everything dependent upon him. Skills and knowledge aside, he was no Leren, as he'd made quite clear. He didn't want the responsibility for Pennebray's life. It wasn't fair to him.

But he'd help. All that he could.

Azrael prepared another dose of the tea and essence of tarrow root, the most powerful painkiller that he knew of. The girl wailed for almost an hour more before she finally quieted. Azrael retreated to his study. Refisal followed.

"Master, you know what you must do," said Refisal. "She will die if you do not."

"There are yet three choices," said Azrael. "There always seems to be three choices."

"Send them away.

"Fill her with pain killers and hope the illness passes before the medicines do her even more harm.

"Or try the serum."

"Though others might, you will not send her away," said Refisal. "You are a man of conscience. You'd never allow a child to die under your watch. That leaves but two choices, and one of those has already failed. The tea has done her little good. The serum remains to be tried."

"I will not have her blood on my hands," said Azrael.

"It healed the mice, the blue serum did," said Refisal

"Mice and little girls are not the same," said Azrael. "Variations of that serum killed most of the mice in the last week. Others it drove mad. Some ran in circles until they dropped dead. The rest banged their heads on the cage until it killed them. Would you have that sweet child end up like that?"

"She's going to die anyway," said Refisal. "In agony, it seems. There's little to lose. Chance it."

"I will not. Let the tea do its work, and then we shall see."

An hour later, the girl was screaming again. They had to hold her down to stop her from pounding her hands against her head.

"You have to try something else," said Lady Cassandra. "Something stronger. There must be another treatment. The pain is killing her. Dear gods, it's killing her."

"No," said Azrael shaking his head.

"Master," said Refisal sharply.

"You have another treatment?" said Lady Cassandra. "I can tell that you do! You must use it. You must! Dear gods, please."

"I cannot experiment on your daughter. She's not a lab rat."

"I will pay you. Anything you want. I have the means — my late husband was Duke Baltan of Farthing Heights. Whatever you desire will be yours. You have only to name it."

"Please, have pity," she said. "Do not let my baby suffer so. Do not let her die. Please."

Azrael shook his head and sighed. "There is a serum—"

"Try it. Try it now. I'll pay you whatever you want."

"I don't want, and won't take your money. The serum is dangerous. That's why I don't want to use it. I've worked on it for many years, but it's not been fully tested."

"Try it. She's dying. Please."

"I need you to understand that if I give it to her, more than likely, the serum itself will kill her."

"If she survives," he said, "she'll likely go mad. She may never again be the girl you know. Do you truly want to take that risk?"

"But there's a chance? A chance that it could cure her? That she could be fine? Healthy again?"

"A chance there is," said Azrael. "But only a small chance."

"Any chance is better than what she's going through now. Do it. Do it now. I can't stand to see her suffer so."

"Are you certain?"

"Yes, do it. Do it now."

Azrael brought down a syringe from the laboratory — an instrument unknown to the people of the area. The girl lay on the big leather couch in the front parlor, moaning, one hand pressed to the side of her head, the other gripped the couch, her knuckles white. Her mother sat beside her, trying unsuccessfully to hold back tears.

Azrael knelt down beside them and had Lady Cassandra remove the girl's shirt. He rubbed a small cloth dipped in iodine on her shoulder, then injected the liquid, a blue-tinted concoction. The girl didn't seem to notice. She made no reaction; her eyes remained closed the whole time.

"What now?" said Lady Cassandra. "How long until she's better?"

"Her fate is in the gods' hands," said Azrael. "I've done all that I could and more than I should have. If the serum works, within a few hours she'll begin to improve."

Azrael paced the room, sipping a brandy for a full half hour. He feared a strong reaction early, and wanted to stay close to the girl's side. But no negative reaction came. After a time, her pain seemed to ease, but whether that was the serum's doing, or the natural course of whatever ailed her, none could say. Eventually she drifted off to a fitful sleep.

Azrael awoke to Refisal's knock on his door. The gnome bowed when he stepped in, his white, pointed beard meticulously groomed as always. He wore his brown suit, with a gray vest and brown tie. He had even combed his hair.

The old dog must have wanted to impress Lady Cassandra. She was nearly twice his height and less than a tenth his age.

A minor deterrence to a determined gnome.

Azrael barely held back a laugh at the very thought of it.

Servants brought water — a pitcher, steaming hot, another chilled with ice, as was customary. They placed them on the sideboard, a towel carefully arranged and folded over to protect the antique wood from any scratches or spills.

"Where is my breakfast?" said Azrael with mock dissatisfaction.

"Downstairs, Master," said a servant.

"Set in the dining hall," said Refisal. "Where you will break your fast with Lady Cassandra and young Miss Pennebray," he said with a smile. So odd a look was the wide, sincere smile on the old gnome's face, that for a moment, Azrael barely recognized him.

"She's awake?"

"Yes, my lord," said a servant.

"Talking non-stop and hungry as a bear in spring," said Refisal. "Downed a pitcher of water and a half loaf of sourdough before I set on my way up here. There was no stopping her. If you don't move quickly, there will be nothing left. You'll be fasting until lunch."

Azrael locked his gaze on Refisal, studying him, trying to discern if this was some jest. When the gnome didn't flinch, Azrael jumped from the bed and marched up to him.

"You did it Master," said Refisal. "You found the cure at last."

"It may only have lessened her illness," said Azrael. "It's too soon to know."

"Her coloring is normal," said Refisal. "No fever. Her grip is as strong as yours. Her mind, sharp despite her ordeal. It's the cure. It has to be. You did it."

Azrael smiled. "Time will tell, but if it's truly the cure, than it's we that did it, old friend. I could not have made the progress I did without your insights. Or at least, it would have taken me a lot longer."

# 26

# THE DEAD FENS, OUTSIDE THE KEEP

*Year 1242, Fourth Age*
*Twelfth Year of King Tenzivel's Rule*

"The Lugron show themselves," whispered Red Tybor.

The keep's portcullis went up slowly, as if to make as little noise as possible. Something was wrong with the mechanism, for it jammed twice along the way. Eventually, several Lugron stepped up and raised it bodily from the inside. When the gate was fully up, a large group of Lugron emerged from the keep, many more than the few that were about when the group arrived.

Most Lugron were average or short in height compared to the men of Lomion, but they were much broader and heavier limbed. They had broad protruding foreheads, heavy brows, and long shaggy unkempt black hair. They wore armor of leather, studded with bronze or iron and ornamented with bones of animals and men.

They peered carefully about as they emerged, focusing on the path that the dead had just traveled. They seemed concerned that more might come from the same direction.

After a few minutes, they appeared to relax and set about to work. Some repaired the big wood doors; others, the portcullis, and still others began construction of a crude barricade outside the entry. Two very tall, burly Lugron barked orders at the others.

"How many?" said Malvegil.

"I count at least sixteen," said Red Tybor.

"Eleven of us," said Ob. "That's not a fair fight at all. Hopefully, they have friends inside to even things up a bit."

"I fear they may have too many friends," said Brother Donnelin.

"I'd like to climb out of this darned ditch and charge straight at them," said Malvegil. "I mark it one hundred fifty yards. Too far. They'll retreat inside long before we get there. Once they drop that portcullis, we're stuck outside, and vulnerable to any archers they might have."

"We wait until dark," said Ob. "Then we can creep up there unseen."

"I doubt that will get us anywhere," said Aradon. "Once they're done with their labors, or night falls, they'll close that gate and maybe the doors if they're repaired. Again, that leaves us stuck outside."

"It does," said Ob. "But we can thief our way in if we put our minds to it. I'm sure of it."

"Not if it's guarded," said Aradon. "They'll raise the alarm and we'll have the whole lot down on us in the dark. Don't forget that they can see in the black better than we can."

"Better than you Volsungs, maybe," said Ob. "Gnomes are famous for our night vision."

"Dwarves too," said McDuff.

"The keep's door faces west," said Gabriel.

"What of it?" said Malvegil.

Ob nodded, a hint of a smile on his face. "We go in at sundown," said Ob. "The light will be in their eyes if they turn toward us."

"So they won't turn, until they hear us," said Aradon. "If we're quiet enough, we might get very close before they see or hear us."

"Or smell us," said Red Tybor. "They're good at that."

"A good plan," said Gabriel. "So long as it isn't too cloudy at dusk. We need that sun on their faces."

"Do we try it?" said Ob.

Aradon and Malvegil both nodded. "We do."

The sun didn't cooperate.

Neither did the fog.

As the day wore on, the sky grew more overcast, but the fog lifted. By late afternoon, the view was clear between the ditch and the castle. Had the ditch not concealed them, the men surely would have been spotted.

"What now?" said Ob.

"We should have charged them earlier when we still had the fog," said Malvegil.

"We wait until morning," said Gabriel. "We jump them when they open the gates."

"How do you know they will?" said Aradon.

"Since so much of the wood they've tried to work with is rotted and falling apart, they're not done repairing the doors," said Gabriel. "They'll be out there again in the morning, assuming they can find some other wood. We'll be waiting. We stay here for the night. And creep up to the wall before dawn. When they come, we jump them, and force our way inside. One way or another, on the morrow, we'll get in there."

# 27

# THE DEAD FENS, OUTSIDE THE KEEP

*Year 1242, Fourth Age
Twelfth Year of King Tenzivel's Rule*

Torbin Malvegil opened his eyes. He was freezing and felt stiff all over. Every inch of his body hurt: sore muscles, top to bottom; back aching; head throbbing; blistered feet. He wasn't used to roughing it quite as much as they'd been doing on that trip. And he hated sleeping on the ground.

Before he got his bearings, Ob thrust a flask in his face.

"Drink it, lordling," said the gnome. "It'll warm your weary bones."

"They're frozen solid," said Malvegil.

"A couple good sips will thaw you. It's gnome mead. Smooth, not like that dwarven swill of McDuff's; this will warm your belly, not burn your throat." Ob sat back against the side of the ditch, hands cupped behind his head. "There's nothing like a cold night in the wild, no fire, no tent, and soaked to the bone. It makes you feel alive, doesn't it?"

"I feel half dead," said Malvegil.

Ob nodded. "Yup. Thought it was just me."

"Your man had a hard night," said Ob gesturing toward Gorlick who lay shivering not far away,

McDuff's flask in hand. Donnelin, McDuff, and Karktan hovered around him; the moons provided just enough light to see them by, the sun not yet up.

"I was afraid of that," said Malvegil. "We should have taken him back at the first sign of infection. I've gotten him killed, haven't I?"

"He's a tough man," said Ob. "Might still make it, though I think he will lose the arm, no matter what we do for him here on out. It's a stinking shame. He's one of the best fighters I've ever seen, and I've seen the best."

"We may have to take it off before we get back," said Ob. "Might be the only way to save his life. Still, it's a terrible thing to do to a man, especially a friend."

"If he doesn't make it, it will be my fault," said Malvegil. "Heck, if he loses his arm, that will be my fault too. He only got bit because he was protecting me."

"I was too slow. I let one get in too close. And Gorlick jumped in to save my butt. If not for my mistake, he would have gotten through that combat clean. It's my fault. As soon as we knew the wound was infected, I should have had us go back."

"You did what you thought was right at the time," said Ob. "And you weren't thinking stupid. You made a rational decision. It turns out that that decision might be wrong. That's one of the burdens of leadership. Get used to it. It's not easy being in charge. Get used that too. You're a lot like your father. You'll do well, just as he did. You've got what it takes. Just keep your head on straight."

"You're a good adviser, gnome."

"I'm just an old scout, past his time, with a lot of opinions."

"A lot of knowledge, you mean. And you're not so old as you pretend to be, at least not for a gnome."

"But my castellan is," said Malvegil. "He's held the post since I was a boy. It's long past time for him to retire. I need a new man in that position. A solid man that will stand with me for many years. I could use you, Mister Ob. It would be a big step up from Master Scout."

"You offering me the job of castellan of Dor Malvegil?"

"Been thinking on it for some time," said Malvegil. "Well before this business came up."

"That's an honor that I'm not sure that I deserve, but I thank you for it," said Ob. "The thing is, I'm an Eotrus man. Served Aradon since he came to power. I served his father before him, and his before him. I've pledged myself to the Eotrus, and with them I will stay until the day that the Valkyries carry me up Valhalla way. That's my answer."

# 28

# THE HOLLOW

*Year 801, Fourth Age*

**A**zrael gave Mikel Potter the injection. A full dose of the serum, pumped into his forearm. Potter didn't flinch. Only forty years old he was, but over the last three years his hands grew crippled with swelling, painful joints that transformed him from the most skilled potter in the district to one that could no longer work at all, for he could not bear the pain. He would never work the clay again.

His apprentices, though competent, had skills that paled in comparison. Potter's business was on the decline, surviving on past reputation alone. Besides his family, his work was his one true love, his calling. His skills and devotion to his trade made him great, and provided his family ample coin and comforts. But now he was broken. Finished. Forced into retirement long before his time. His business slipping away. Slowly. But in the end, he'd lose it all. All he'd worked for. His children's future. He wanted so much for them not to need to toil away their lives as he had. He wanted to give them a good life. A happy life. An easier life. Now that dream was dead.

No healing could help his hands. No herbalist's ointment, no alchemist's potion. No rest or exercise. Some treatments worked for a time, but they didn't last. It broke him, that disease did, not only of body, but also of heart, mind, and spirit.

But Azrael had the cure. He could restore the potter to the man that he once was, and so much more. And that was his plan.

The potter was the last of the group of ten that Azrael had chosen. All young or middle-aged. All suffering or broken in some serious way. The baker, the sheepherder, the coinmaster, two servants, the cook, and more. Some were near death from illness or accident.

Azrael picked the ten carefully, selecting those that were the most in need and the most worthy, as best he could judge.

If the serum remained potent and the patients' symptoms were forever banished, he'd be able to help everyone.

To save everyone.

To cure the great plague once and for all.

But he had to go slow.

He had to do it smart. He knew full well that he might have to tweak the formula to reduce any negative effects.

Or, more likely, provide a second injection, or perhaps, repeated, periodic injections. Maybe for weeks. Or years. Or forever. But those were details. The cure was in hand.

Azrael had never experimented on anyone before in his quest for the cure, not in all the years that he had sought it. Only the animals died for it. Mice mostly, more than he could ever count. Azrael was a man of weighty conscience, so that even the experimentation on animals weighed heavily on him.

It took time, a great deal of time, but he

hardened himself to it.

He had too.

For without the animal testing, he could make little progress. The cure would have remained unfound for all time.

Limiting his work to animal testing made it harder — infinitely harder — but there was no human cost.

No tearing at his soul.

And so that's how he had to proceed. It was not his nature to cause pain or harm to anyone. To play with or belittle their lives. That was against all that he stood for. That's why, so long ago, he joined the rebellion against the lord. That's why he joined with Thetan, Mithron, Gabriel, and the others.

And where their cabal sought only to protect the innocent, they were confounded, for what they did, the actions they took, the rebellion they fostered, brought about pain a thousandfold times worse upon humanity than anything Azathoth ever did.

That guilt had weighed on him, down through the long years. It had driven him to spend all his days seeking a cure.

That was his penance.

He had to atone for what he'd done, though he'd not intentionally harmed any innocents. It was his actions, and the actions of the other traitors that had brought about the plague. That had caused infinite suffering and death upon humanity. He often wondered, long and hard, had the lord been in the right?

Were they in the wrong?

Did they fail to see the bigger picture?
The greater good?
The divine plan?
Had they ruined everything? Were they truly the traitors that history had painted them?

Those thoughts were never far from Azrael's mind. But the answers were elusive. Or rather, not definitive. It was, unknowable.

Only by knowing the lord's mind would they ever know the truth. And the lord was gone from Midgaard, and the truth with him. All they had left was the plague and its consequences.

Azrael had foregone most of the pleasures of life in his single-minded pursuit of the cure. Of atonement. Of a forgiveness that could never be attained. That could never be granted. For the people didn't even know what he, what they, had done.

No one remembered.
No one knew.

It was too long ago. His crimes not forgiven, but forgotten. The people didn't even know that the plague existed. That they were suffering from it. That it was killing them all.

He could have given up. He could have sought a life, some happiness. Some semblance of family and normalcy. But he wouldn't. He couldn't. Never. Not so long as there was a chance for a cure. And that chance, however small, was what kept him going. It fueled the fire of his heart. It made life worth living.

Without that hope. Without that goal, looming out there, somewhere beyond his reach, he would have long ago given up.

He'd have ended his existence.
He would have been forgotten in the fullness of time, just as were all his brethren.

# 29

# THE DEAD FENS, OUTSIDE THE KEEP

*Year 1242, Fourth Age*
*Twelfth Year of King Tenzivel's Rule*

Before the first light of dawn, as one, the men crept up the side of the ditch, concealed by the dark. So deep was the black, that they couldn't even see the keep. The ground was uneven, rocky, and muddy. Malvegil called for them to crawl, but Aradon called that off straightaway. If not him, Gabriel would have done the same.

"On our bellies, we'll be spent by the time we get there," said Aradon.

So they crouched low and made their way forward by twos. They took up position against the keep's wall to one side of the entrance, out of sight of anyone that might look through the door.

Tight against the wall, no one could see them from what few windows the keep had. Unless some silent sentinel had spotted them, their plan had thus far worked.

As they waited, Gabriel decided they needed a decoy. Ob and Par Talbon got the duty. They were to lie down on the ground some fifty yards from the entrance in full sight of the door. After the Lugron opened the portcullis, it was Ob's job to get their attention and draw them out. Talbon was there to back Ob up, employing whatever magics that were called for. This tactic was needed, otherwise, it may be that the first Lugron that came out the door would spot the men and run for it.

They needed to draw them out.

"The gnome and the wizard are in position," said Red Tybor. "Your plan?" he said to Malvegil.

"We plow through the Lugron and then on to whoever or whatever is within," said Malvegil. "We must be certain that once that portcullis goes up, it stays up until we're all inside."

"Shore it with timbers?" said Red Tybor. "The wagon may serve," he said pointing to an old wagon that lay beside the keep's wall, two wheels missing.

"Karktan and Donnelin," said Malvegil. "You've got the duty. As soon as we engage the Lugron, get that wagon pulled under the portcullis as swiftly as you can. We don't want half of us in and half out."

"We must be swift whatever the risks," said Gabriel. "We can't give the Lugron's master time to gather his strength." Gabriel looked over to Gorlick.

"I am with you," said Gorlick, his voice shaky. From when they'd awoken, his condition had continued to decline. His color, mottled; his face, drawn and sweaty despite the chill in the air.

"You should rest," said Gabriel. "You need to save your strength. One sword more or less will not carry the day or end us."

"Time enough to rest when I'm dead," said

Gorlick. "I would die on my feet in battle with a sword in my hand, my friends and comrades at my side. I've no interest in dying alone, lying in a muddy hole. I may end this day in Valhalla, but I'll send some stinking Lugron to Helheim first."

"Aradon," said Malvegil, "I trust you've given Talbon and Donnelin leave to use their magics?"

"They are so permitted," said Aradon. "With no restrictions."

The men gathered close together, shoulder to shoulder, and Brother Donnelin led them in a whispered battle prayer, an ancient tradition of their people. Each man bowed his head and whispered their words. Words that spoke of duty, honor, and glory. Each man knew every line by heart.

"To victory and tomorrow if we can, to victory and Valhalla if we must," whispered the men as the prayer concluded. "This we vow."

Some of them believed that the gods were listening; some thought the gods didn't care; some didn't believe in the gods at all, but they spoke their words just the same.

## 30

# THE DEAD FENS, OUTSIDE THE KEEP

*Year 1242, Fourth Age
Twelfth Year of King Tenzivel's Rule*

"Faster you scum," bellowed Gorgorath, a massive one-eyed Lugron, graybearded and grizzled, with corded muscles the size of tree trunks for arms. In his broad hand he gripped an iron axe twice as heavy as most men wielded; a barbed whip hung from his belt. "Get that gate up," he shouted.

A few moments later, the portcullis rose before him, but it paused, shuddered, and threatened to jam with every few inches of progress. He heard the men on the wheel shouting to each other, grunting and straining in attempt to keep it moving. Some of that was for show; they feared his wrath, as well they should, but he knew that they were doing their best, lazy scum that they were; he had to give them that, for the darned mechanism was a rusted ruin — decayed from ages of moisture and neglect. He'd had the boys working on it for two weeks straight with little progress; no surprise since there wasn't a decent tinker or blacksmith amongst them. Good fighters were his men, but as far as thinking, not so much.

That was his department, the thinking. Him

and Grontor; not that the boy knew much yet, but he had potential.

Lots of potential.

As his father, that made him proud.

Gorgorath would've given up on the gate long ago if not for the draugar (the Lugron name for the shamblers). The wooden doors couldn't hold them back, not nearly; they just kept tearing them down. So he had the bulk of his men on repair duty every day. What barricades they could build weren't any more effective than the doors, though they were better than nothing.

It didn't help that the sappers were all dead, so even carpentry and masonry work was a stretch for the boys what were left; they made due, though. Self-preservation and Gorgorath's whip being more than sufficient motivations.

Only the iron portcullis afforded true protection. It was strong despite its age and flakey rust. Solid iron bars an inch and a half around, closely spaced, and as heavy as a frost giant's heel. The draugar would never get through it; not that gate. So Gorgorath needed to get it into working order. He needed to be able to raise and lower it with speed when the draugar came calling, which was all too frequently. Persistent buggers were they; kept coming back for reasons unknown. At night mostly, but in the daytime too.

With the keep's basement now fully flooded (and the side and rear doors down there under water), the main gate was the only practical way in and out of the keep. The windows on the main levels and above amounted to little more than arrow slits — too narrow for a man to get through.

The only windows big enough to get out of were up high. It would take ropes and climbing to get down from there. In a pinch, they could get out that way, but not every day. The main gate had to be kept clear and in working order.

And without the barrier that the portcullis provided, Gorgorath knew that he and his would likely all get dead. It didn't matter that all his men were professional soldiers; more than a few highly skilled, for the draugar were hard to put down.

They had no fear, did the draugar.

They were relentless.

Imagine that, Gorgorath's Bonebreakers, the most famed and feared Lugron mercenary company in all the Southlands (as the Lugron called everywhere south of the Kronar Range), wiped out by a bunch of dead things out of ancient legend. Would've been funny to Gorgorath if it had happened to some other company. Why not Wolfrick and his scum? They deserved such a fate. The Bonebreakers didn't.

One way or another, their assignment couldn't last much longer. Things had spiraled out of control after the draugar got loose. Since then, they'd killed half his company; most of them in the chaos of that first day. That scared his men shitless. And who could blame them?

Gorgorath had seen a lot in his day. Things that made brave men flee, cry, pee themselves, and puke, but he'd never seen anything quite like the draugar. They never tired. They never gave up. They had no concept of mercy. And they felt no pain. Qualities Gorgorath admired in his men; not so much in his enemies.

It didn't help that the warlock was a madman. That was no shock. Gorgorath saw that from the first, but it didn't matter none, since he had plenty of silver, and was ready to part with it.

The problem was, the warlock had gotten a lot worse of late, or else maybe he just stopped hiding his lunacy. If not for the silver, Gorgorath would've long since pulled his Bonebreakers out. But seeing how it would be a difficult slog to get clear of the Fens with the draugar roaming about out there, Gorgorath planned to hold out a bit longer. He figured that soon enough the warlock would order them to take another ship and bring back more captives. When he did, Gorgorath planned to demand a heap of silver up front to do the deed. Once pocketed, he'd take the whole company out, what remained of it anyways, head for the eastern hills, and never look back.

Assuming they got clear, there wasn't much downside to the plan. The warlock wasn't about to track down the company all on his lonesome, looking to collect back his silver, and exact revenge.

There would be better jobs for the company elsewhere. Cleaner doings than what the warlock and the Fens had to offer.

It would take a darned long time though to rebuild the company back to what it had been. But it had to be done. The only good part being, with so many Bonebreakers dead, each surviving man got a much larger share of pay.

Especially Gorgorath.

Not enough to retire on, not by a long stretch, but a good heap of coin all the same. Gorgorath figured that he had a few more good years in him at the least. And Grontor was still learning. Had to finish schooling him up so that he could take over the company one day and do him proud.

# 31

# THE HOLLOW, AZRAEL'S MANOR

*Year 801, Fourth Age*

"Master, there are other ill folk in town," said Refisal. "Many more could benefit from this treatment. Old folks too — suffering from the infirmities of age."

"Ten is enough for now," said Azrael. "And too many if the cure proves false. I wish that we could help everyone in need. But we can't. Not yet. Not until we know for certain that the cure is sound, lasting, and of no ill consequence. We don't know that yet. Not for certain. For all we know, the child's ailment may yet return, perhaps worse than it was. The others too. Imagine that? How will I feel then? How will I face them? What will I say to Lady Cassandra?"

The gnome didn't immediately respond. He didn't seem to have any answers.

"The thought of bringing about such suffering weighs heavily on me, night and day," said Azrael. "So too does the idea of withholding the cure until the testing is complete. If it proves sound, then every day, every moment, that I kept it from the needy, unnecessarily prolonged their suffering. In a way, it makes me responsible for that suffering. There is no good choice in this matter."

"Then mayhap the best choice might be to ease your burden, and give the cure freely to all and everyone," said Refisal. "If it's not lasting and requires additional treatments, we can deal with that. We can forewarn them that that may be the case, so no one is surprised."

"What of potential side effects?" said Azrael.

"How likely is it that any will be worse than their main ailments?"

"Not likely," said Azrael.

"It's been twelve days and Lady Cassandra reports her daughter is well," said Refisal. "So is Ebert Cook, who you treated three days later. The cure is sound, Master." Refisal paused, saying nothing further, letting Azrael think.

"Your words are wise, as always, my friend," said Azrael. "But I will not chance it. I will not gamble with the lives or the health of any beyond those few that we have already treated. Not until we know for certain that the cure is all that we hope it to be. If fate causes pain or suffering or takes the lives of others in the meanwhile, such be the will of the higher powers, if any such powers yet exist."

"So be it, my master," said Refisal.

"Continue to check in with the patients every few days. Report any ill effects to me, however minor."

"Of course," said Refisal. "But for how long?"

"One month," said Azrael. "If in one month from today, no patient has relapsed and none suffer untoward effects attributable to the serum, we shall begin to administer it freely. In the meantime, we will hope for the best, and purchase the equipment and supplies that we'll need to mass-produce the serum. When the month is up, we'll be ready to go."

"An exciting time, Master," said Refisal.

"Aye," said Azrael. "If all goes as we hope, we will change the world. All of Midgaard will be saved."

"Saved from a plague they know not that they suffer from," said Refisal. "How ironic."

## 32

# THE DEAD FENS, OUTSIDE THE KEEP

*Year 1242, Fourth Age
Twelfth Year of King Tenzivel's Rule*

Gorgorath looked past the portcullis's bars. A cold morning. That cold held down the bog's stench and that was a good thing. And the morning was clearer than usual. Not much fog. They'd see the draugar coming from farther away. That would make it safer than it had been in a while.

With luck, and sharp watchmen on duty, perhaps he wouldn't lose any men that day. That would be a good thing. There were far too many losses of late.

So far at least, no draugar were in sight. Unlike the previous few days, his crew was going to get an early start on their work. Maybe they'd finally get the darned barricade completed and reinforced enough that it would hold. That would keep the draugar well back from the doors and the portcullis and give them another much-needed line of defense.

"You heard the captain," boomed Grontor, Gorgorath's young lieutenant. Taller and broader of shoulder even than his father, Grontor was leaner and quicker. "Get that gate up! And be ready to drop it on orders. Those scum may show up any moment."

The gate up, Gorgorath stepped out into the morning light, spearmen on his flanks, the others huddled close behind him — two full squadrons, sixty men in total, the iron core of what remained of the Bonebreakers. They'd gotten jumped by the draugar more than once in the morning, so they were wary and moved about in force. In the morning especially, they took no chances.

To Gorgorath's surprise, he heard a voice on the breeze, coming from somewhere out in the bog. It spoke some words, then paused, then spoke again. A living person's voice, not the croaking call of the draugar. What it said, he couldn't make out.

It made no sense. How could anyone be out there, this deep in the Fens, and with the draugar roaming? He looked about, but didn't see anyone.

Was the voice real? His imagination? Or some will-o'-the-wisp?

And then he wondered if it could be one of his men. They weren't all accounted for. Not since the draugar had overrun the place.

Then Gorgorath spied a strange little character waving its arms and jumping up and down some fifty yards out. It was its voice that spoke.

It called out again. It sounded like it was asking for help, but Gorgorath still couldn't make out its words. Its accent was thick. For certain, it was no Lugron. So, not one of his men.

"What's that little fellow doing skulking about the bog?" muttered Gorgorath.

"What is it?" said one of the spearmen, a

young Lugron called Tribik. An imbecile, but loyal. "Some kind of dwarf?"

"Must be," said Gorgorath. "No Volsung is that small. A female dwarf, by the look. You can tell because she doesn't have much of a beard. Keep your eyes peeled for any sign of draugar. We don't need them sneaking up on us while we're dealing with Little Lady Dwarf. She might be running from them."

"Looks clear," said Tribik, though he barely looked around at all, his attention fixed on the "dwarf".

"They took my gold," shouted the dwarf. "They robbed me. Please help me. Can you help me?"

"Did she say gold?" asked Gorgorath.

"No, she said that she's cold," said Tribik. "Maybe give her a blanket or some hot spiced tea?"

"She's got a sword," said another Lugron. "She looks dangerous."

"All dwarves carry weapons," said Gorgorath. "They're always looking for trouble, they are. Vicious little things. They'll kill you as soon as look at you. But no need to flee just yet, so pull your tail out from between your legs. I think we can handle one little dwarf girl, don't you?"

"They didn't get all of it," said the dwarf as she held up a money purse and ambled closer to their position. That purse clearly held more than a few coins.

The dwarf was rich.

"Please, can you help me to get the rest of my gold back? There's a reward in it for you, if we get it. A big one," she said, jiggling the money purse.

"Please, I can't do it alone."

"Should we help her, captain?" said Tribik. "She's asking all nice and proper, showing us respect and all. And she might be pretty. I think she is," he said, squinting.

"We may have to help her," said Gorgorath. "We can't have somebody running around the bog robbing people under our noses. This is our territory. If there's any robbing to be done, we'll be doing it, not nobody else. Hopefully, it's just some of our boys what nicked her gold; some that got clear of the draugar and are hold up out in the bog somewhere."

"Captain," said Tribik, "isn't this the warlock's territory, not ours?"

"That's what I said," said Gorgorath. "Set your ears on straight, you sniveling moron."

Tribik fiddled with both his ears, one after the other, straightening them as best he could. Tribik's face scrunched up as they marched closer to Ob. "I was wrong, captain," he said. "She's butt ugly. Almost as bad as them elves. Look at the size of her nose."

"All dwarves are ugly," said Gorgorath. "Especially the women."

"That's a shame," said Tribik. "Would've been nice to see a pretty face."

"Aye," said Gorgorath. "That would have been nice, indeed." That's when he heard the battle cries from the rear. "Shit!" he said. "They've jumped us. Turn about. Stand together."

# 33

# THE DEAD FENS, OUTSIDE THE KEEP

*Year 1242, Fourth Age*
*Twelfth Year of King Tenzivel's Rule*

Gorgorath was very tall for a Lugron. Taller and broader than all but two or three of his men, them being giants amongst their kind, so he could see easily enough over the others. He saw some of what was coming at them. And it wasn't draugar.

Some were Volsungs for certain. Some others, he wasn't certain of. A strange crew. Different races; different sizes of men. Mercs. They had to be. Just like his Bonebreakers.

Gorgorath figured that someone must have missed one of them ships they pirated or the folks what was on them. So they went and hired up some sell swords to go a-looking for them. Maybe for rescuing. Maybe for revenge. Maybe both. They'd be tough, them mercs. Their kind always was. It would be a battle. Fierce and bloody.

At least the numbers were on his side. They outmanned the mercs four or five to one, maybe more, unless there was more of them hidden about. And his crew were armed and armored to the teeth. The Bonebreakers had been in tough fights before. Plenty of times. They always came out on top. This time would be no different.

Gorgorath just had to make certain that not too many of his men got killed. The Bonebreakers couldn't afford that. Many more losses and they'd be out of business. All the warlock's silver wasn't worth that.

Gorgorath saw a bronze-skinned savage leap into the air, spear in hand. Lean but muscled, the man's arms were bare despite the cold. A small round clump of black hair pulled to a ponytail sat atop his head, the rest shaved bald.

A Pict.

Gorgorath hated Picts.

The Pict skewered old Trench with that spear. Stabbed him through the neck — a mortal wound. Trench was old and slow. Not a fighter at all; he was their cook. A gentle man. Never had a chance. Not against a wild man like that Pict. And now he was dying. For what?

Gorgorath would make them pay, them mercs. He'd make them bleed. He'd make them beg for death before he was through with them. Especially the Pict, that evil bastard.

## 34

## THE HOLLOW

*Year 801, Fourth Age*

**A**zrael walked down the alley, his tall, wide-brimmed hat, long gray cloak, oversized walking stick, and polished black boots announcing his presence louder than a town crier. He wore no armor, at least none that was visible, but there was no mistaking the sword tip that jutted through a slit in his cloak. The handle of another blade stuck up from behind his right shoulder. He moved at a measured pace, but his long strides covered ground faster than Refisal could easily match. The old gnome jogged along behind his master, sucking in air as he went, though he never fell far behind.

Three men awaited them halfway down the alley. There was a body on the ground near them. Other men stood at the alley's far end where it met the next street.

"The tenth in five days," said Mayor Barnton to Azrael, his face grim.

Azrael looked confused. "There were seven victims as of last night."

"Three more so far tonight," said the mayor. "Two servants inside, and their mistress, here," he said pointing to the body. "The seamstress next door heard the screams and sent her eldest boy out the front to get the constable."

"I had two men here within as many minutes," said the constable. "The fiend was still at work."

"They saw him?" said Azrael. "Was it the dwarf?"

"No, it was no dwarf," said the third man, one of the marshals. "The killer was as tall as you. And as broad."

"The witnesses to the previous murders claimed the killer was short, sleight — a thin dwarf, maybe even a tall gnome," said Azrael.

"That's not what I saw," said the marshal. "I saw a very tall Volsung man. No dwarf or gnome was he. Not by his height. Not by his breadth. No chance of it."

"Could we have two killers?" said the mayor.

"Before this started, there were no murders in The Hollow since I was a boy," said the constable. "Even then, it was over some feud; never random like this. I don't believe that two killers have come to town at the same time. I won't accept that."

"Unless they're working together," said the mayor.

"A tall Volsung and a dwarf," said the marshal. "Or a gnome."

Azrael's eyes narrowed when he saw the marshal looking him and Refisal up and down.

"Where were you earlier tonight?" said the marshal.

"Don't be an idiot," said the mayor.

"There are few men in town as tall as he," said the constable. "So it's a fair question."

"Master Azrael is our best chance at stopping the fiend," said the mayor. "He's not the killer. He's one of us; an upstanding citizen of many years."

"I came here at your request, gentlemen," said Azrael. "It was your man that roused me and mine from our beds, beseeching aid. Now you accuse me? All because of height? Have you lost your senses?"

"Perhaps we have all lost our senses after the terrible events of the past nights," said the mayor. "I apologize for the good marshal's words. He's scared. We all are. The Hollow has never suffered through anything like this before. It's outside our experience. The savagery of it. It's inhuman. We called you here to help us, not to stand accused of anything. You have my sincerest apologies."

Azrael stepped past the men and looked down at the body. An older woman, her throat torn out.

Refisal moved to his side. "Bitten at neck and wrists, just like the others. But otherwise, her body is untouched."

"As I said, my men caught the killer in the act," said the constable. "He ran for it before he was done. The servants inside have similar wounds, but their torsos are gnawed upon. Bits missing. Who could do that? And to what end?"

"He took more time with them," said Refisal. "Inside, away from prying eyes."

"The old woman must have walked in on it," said Azrael. "When the killer saw her, he gave chase, and finished her here in the alley."

Azrael squatted and put a hand on the body. "Still warm."

"Less than an hour ago, she fell," said the marshal.

Azrael studied the bloodstains on the cobblestones. So too did he study the bodies of the servants within the home.

"Has anyone touched the bodies," said Azrael. "Moved them? Turned them over? Anything?"

"We left everything exactly as we found it," said the marshal.

"Just as with the previous victims," said the constable, "the doors were opened for the killer. He did not break in."

"As if the killer was known to the victims," said Azrael.

"If that is true," said the mayor, "then the killer is one of us, a local. Who amongst us would do such a thing? And why?"

"Who indeed?" said the marshal, still eying Azrael suspiciously.

"The answer lies in the connection between the victims," said Azrael.

"What connection do you mean?" said the constable. "The first few victims were homeless or poor folk. The rest, wealthy folk. Two groups that rarely mix. I see no connection."

"Once we find the connection, we'll find the killer, or killers," said Azrael.

"So you do think that there is more than one?" said the mayor.

"I fear so, yes," said Azrael.

## 35

## THE DEAD FENS, OUTSIDE THE KEEP

*Year 1242, Fourth Age*
*Twelfth Year of King Tenzivel's Rule*

**G**orgorath heard a crackle of electricity bearing down on him from behind, from where the dwarf woman was.

The little bitch was a stinking sorcerer.

Gorgorath dropped to the ground and pulled Tribik down with him — not because he cared a lick about the idiot, he just happened to be right next to him.

The wave of mystical energy roared over them, crackling, buzzing, and popping as it branched out and hunted down its victims.

The magic exploded around them.

His men screamed.

Some of the agonized cries cut off immediately, others droned on and on — the men burned crispy, but not dead, though soon to be. The smell of burnt flesh hung heavy in the air.

A score of men went down from that one shot. Nearly a full squadron. Felled in an instant. A hard day already for the Bonebreakers, and the battle was just getting started.

Gorgorath bounced up, ready to charge the sorcerer, to cut off her stinking head for what she'd done to his men, but Old Mog, the company's battle mage, was on her.

Reliable Old Mog.

She looked the part. A horned helmet, bone earrings, necklace, and belt. Robes with pockets aplenty. A cowl that covered her face and that she rarely took off. A snarling, raspy voice, and a disposition to match. That was Mog. Thirty years with the company. They'd had other wizards along the way, hedges mostly, a couple legit, but they all got dead eventually, most within a year of signing on. Old Mog outlasted them all.

She was a killer. Tough as nails. Afraid of nothing short of a grandmaster from the Tower of the Arcane. She'd make that dwarf bitch burn.

Mog said her mystic words, and spit some foul-smelling ichor from her mouth. Her usual bunk. Then she launched her spell. But not just any incantation. She threw her death magic.

Gorgorath didn't expect that. He cringed when he saw what she conjured, but was happy all the same — his revenge at hand. He thought that she'd throw that flimsy fiery thing she used all the time, what burnt up a man or two, or more when she got lucky. Or else maybe that other spell what sparked all silver and white and knocked men unconscious, sometimes scrambling their brains. Instead, straight off, at the start of the battle, she threw her worst. In thirty years, she'd never done that before. Not once.

The boys called that spell the *dead fog*.

It was akin to some amorphous, otherworldly creature out of your worst nightmare — a wispy shadow of innumerable black tendrils; their touch, near instant death. When they grabbed hold of you, they wouldn't let go. Not ever. They strangled you, pulled the air straight out of your lungs, and sucked the juices from your veins. When the *dead fog* was done with you, all that was left was a flyaway heap of desiccated skin and bones. Barely enough worth burying.

The *dead fog* could take out whole squadrons of men in but seconds. An evil magic it was, without mercy.

But it did discriminate.

It had a presence to it — almost a personality, as if it were alive. As if it were an intelligent creature, not just random energy pulled down from the weave and focused by Mog's skills. It chose its victims, the *dead fog* did, passing over some few, for reasons unknown, devouring all the rest. A will of its own, it had. A plan and a purpose. What they were, no mortal knew.

Not even Old Mog.

A wicked thing, that magic. Rarely used. And rightly so.

It shot from her hands, that black fog did, and grew larger as it went — spreading out, a hundred snakelike tendrils darting and flopping about, searching for victims, hunting for souls.

Mog pulled it down from the blackest corners of the weave — from the places more civilized wizards would never tread. She didn't fear it though, that dark magic. She was at home with it, but never took it lightly; never turned her back on it, for she knew it would turn on her at the first opportunity. It would feast on her soul as quickly as it dined on anyone else's.

You couldn't look straight at the black tendrils — they made your eyes sting and started you coughing, sometimes even spitting up blood. Just from looking at them!

Look away, though, and you'd be fine, so long as they didn't touch you. If they did, you got dead. And that was that. Gorgorath never asked Mog why just looking at it got you sick; he didn't want to even think on it. And truth be told, Gorgorath didn't much like talking to Old Mog. She scared him, though he'd never admit that to anyone. Maybe not even to himself.

But Old Mog knew.

And Gorgorath knew that she knew. They had an understanding, they did.

He'd only seen her use that spell a half dozen times. Mog kept it in reserve for when they were badly outnumbered or when they faced a wizard of true power. Even then, she held it back unto the last. It was too dark, too dangerous, even for her. But not this time.

After that magical blast fried crispy so many Bonebreakers, Old Mog must have realized she faced something worse than her that day. Someone more powerful than she'd ever faced before. So she threw her best, first — all her power behind it.

To Gorgorath's surprise, it wasn't the dwarf woman that was Old Mog's opponent. Next to that pathetic shrimp stood a spindly Volsung clad all in black. He looked like a caricature of a Hand assassin. An evil visage did he have. To Gorgorath's eyes, he appeared from nowhere. Like a dark spectre called up from the Nether

Realms. One moment, the dwarf bitch stood alone. The next, the sorcerer was there, at her side, to do her bidding, or perhaps, she to do his.

Any fool would have ran from the *dead fog*, them black tendrils coming at them. Or else dived to the ground and hoped for the best, praying to their gods to spare them or else call them home quick like.

But not that spindly wizard out of Helheim. He stood his ground. No fear on his face.

All he did was lift his hand up, palm outward, as Mog's magic came in. Just that slight gesture, nothing more.

That hand. Even at a distance, Gorgorath could see it was bony, skeletal. A horrid, misshapen thing. He reached out with it, the dark wizard did, and by some unholy magic, some dark conjuring known only to the Volsungs, he sucked that *dead fog* straight out of the air. Sucked it out.

Straight into his hand.

Took control of it, he did, that evil bastard.

Mastered it. Bested it.

Bent it to *his* will. Made it his thing. Just like that, without even breaking a sweat.

It went into his hand slow at first — a single tendril got sucked in, but then more. After a few moments, Mog's entire fogbank sped toward the dark wizard's palm and got sucked down into nothingness, the opposite of how it came out of Mog's hand.

Old Mog pulled back her cowl to get a better look, disbelieving her eyes. Her face was deathly pale, pretty in its way, despite the sparse beard and all the scars. Her eyes were filled with fear.

Gorgorath had never seen her afraid before. Not once.

A moment later, the *dead fog* roared back at Old Mog, wailing like a banshee as it sprang from the black hole at the center of the wizard's skeletal palm. It was not Mog's spell any longer. Now the tendrils were red as blood; its main mass, an opaque sea of crimson. Now it was the dark wizard's magic. His spawn. Under his control.

Startled as she was, Old Mog spat out some wizard words — a protective enchantment. She didn't panic and toss out just any old incantation. She kept her wits about her and threw the best she had, or at least, the best that she could call up quick. Her fingers wiggled; her hands motioned this way and that. A fiery shield of silver materialized before her, taller than she, it was, and six foot wide at least — a mystic barrier of sufficient power to stop a giant in its tracks, or repel an angry archwizard's spell.

It did her no good.

One red tendril darted up and over the shield, unhindered. It wrapped around Old Mog's neck and lifted her up, into the air, squealing and kicking. It pulled her toward that crimson abyss, that mass of amorphous death that wriggled and hungered before her.

Old Mog struggled. She fought like a demon. She spouted curses that made Gorgorath's ears burn and his hair stand on end. Sparks flew from her fingertips. Balls of mystic energy streamed from her hands. Fire spouted from her mouth. She blew pieces off the tendrils. Her magic ripped them. Tore them. Obliterated them. Burnt them to ash.

It did no good.

The red fog swallowed Old Mog. It ate her up and left little behind. Her gnarled old staff, her horned helmet, and all them bone accoutrements went with her. All gone. That dark magic sucked out her soul and devoured it. Gorgorath saw it all, powerless to intervene in a duel of wizards.

Gorgorath saw one of the crimson tendrils passed into Old Mog's chest, all magic-like, not even breaking the skin, but somehow getting in. Then Gorgorath saw a shadow, like a silhouette of Old Mog, get pulled clean out of her chest by that red tendril thing.

Maybe it was her soul. Maybe her spirit. Her essence. Gorgorath didn't know. Such things were beyond him. But whatever it was, spirit or soul or whatnot, it didn't come out easy. It fought the tendrils for every inch. But they were too strong.

One tendril held the shadow of Mog, another held her body. Them evil things put her body face to face with her spirit.

They taunted her.

The evil magic let her know what it was about to do. It made her watch as other tendrils swooped in — ones with black mouths and ragged teeth. They ripped into the spirit Mog, tearing large chunks out of it.

Old Mog screamed and writhed as she watched it, reacting to each bite, but helpless to do anything. Anything except scream.

The *red fog* made her watch her soul get eaten. Devoured. It only took a few moments, such was the tendrils' hunger, but it felt like forever. When the spirit Mog was gone, the tendrils set to sucking the life from her mortal body, Mog screaming the whole time. When it was done, all that was left of Old Mog was a shriveled desiccated husk. Only then did the *red fog* vanish back whence it came.

Gorgorath could hardly believe his eyes. What a horror that was to see. What a blasphemy. An evil deed the like of which he and the Bonebreakers had never done. Never seen done. Mog's spell never did that to its victims. Not like that.

What sort of men were they facing that commanded such evil magics? And of such frightful power? Perhaps not men at all. That's when the Lugron captain knew that what they faced that day outside the warlock's keep was pure evil.

Better perhaps to name them monsters than men.

Fiends.

Devils.

Old Mog was the best there was. The most powerful wizard that Gorgorath had ever seen. But she was far outclassed by that spindly Volsung thing. And she got dead for it.

Gorgorath would not let her stand unavenged. He felt the adrenalin rush through his body. He'd fight. He'd not stop fighting until these bastards were dead or Old Death took him. He'd fight them to the bitter end.

But after what happened to Old Mog, deep down, Gorgorath knew the terrible, bitter truth. This was the Bonebreaker's final battle.

His final battle.

# 36

# THE HOLLOW

*Year 801, Fourth Age*

"You know more than you told the mayor and the lawmen, Master," said Refisal, as he and Azrael walked toward home through the dark streets of The Hollow.

"Did you see the stains on the cobblestones near the old woman's neck and wrists?" said Azrael.

Refisal shook his head.

"The smears of blood on the wood floor, around the servants' bodies?"

"That I noticed."

"There lies the true horror of this."

"I don't follow, Master," said Refisal.

"You vex me, gnome," said Azrael shaking his head. "In some ways, you are the smartest, most knowledgeable man I've known, and in other ways, you are blind. You fail to make the connection between things that should be obvious to a man of your intellect."

"I stand at once complemented and insulted," said Refisal. "The mayor, the constable, and the others — they too failed to see whatever it is you're alluding to."

"They are common men, with common limitations. You are different. I expect more from you. I need you to think, to evaluate what we saw, not just to accept it at face value. Think it through, from every angle, just as you do with our experiments. I need you to take that same approach with everything. It will make you infinitely more valuable to me."

"I will endeavor to do as you suggest," said Refisal.

"So I ask you again about the blood," said Azrael. "What was odd about it?"

"That there wasn't more of it?" said Refisal.

"Exactly," said Azrael. "On the cobbles, we saw brown stains only. No pooled blood. Not a single drop. Yet the murder occurred but forty minutes prior, and the stains prove that she bled there, at that very spot, just as the marshal reported. What does that tell you?"

"The killer cleaned up the blood before the marshals arrived," said Refisal. "To what end?"

"He didn't clean it up," said Azrael. "Nor did he collect it in some vessel and spirit it away."

"Then what?"

"He drank it."

"Lapped it up straight off the cobbles," said Azrael. "I missed that fact with the earlier bodies because they weren't discovered until the following day. I thought that the blood dried up, or that dogs or other animals got at it, even though the scenes lacked footprints of the same. Not figuring that out sooner was a blunder. My blunder. But now we know."

"He drinks the blood?" said Refisal. "How disgusting. And aberrant. Why do such a thing?"

"Why indeed?" said Azrael. "And not "he," but rather, "they." If the eyewitness reports hold any validity at all, then we're dealing with at least two killers here. Perhaps more. Killers that drink blood. That hunt people for blood. And that gnaw upon them. Eating their flesh. This is something new, Refisal. Something I haven't seen before."

# 37

# THE DEAD FENS, OUTSIDE THE KEEP

*Year 1242, Fourth Age
Twelfth Year of King Tenzivel's Rule*

Gorgorath tore his eyes away from Old Mog's husk when the spearman next to him howled in pain and staggered forward. Gorgorath spun around and saw the dwarf woman's bloody axe slicing through the air.

Up close, he wasn't certain that the dwarf was a female. But with dwarves, how can you really tell?

And it didn't matter. Not anymore. He was going to kill her, or him, or it, or whatever it was, and that would be that. He might die in this battle, but not to a stinking dwarf.

Before Gorgorath brought his sword to bear, the dwarf's axe came at him. The little bugger was so quick. She moved like lightning. Gorgorath deflected the strike off the iron bracer he wore on his forearm. He'd done as much many times before, but never against so powerful a blow. His left arm went numb and useless. How the little thing had such strength, he couldn't fathom.

Gorgorath's sword caught the dwarf's second swing and deflected it aside, sparks flying.

The dwarf's axe came in again and again,

slicing this way and that, powerful strokes, carefully aimed, precisely timed. She was an expert, a seasoned veteran of the killing game. And she'd done her job well, distracted them but good, letting her fellows sneak up on them from behind. Caught the Bonebreakers unawares. Right into a trap. Not many were savvy enough to do that.

Gorgorath would make her pay. For he was an expert too. Thirty years of soldiering under Brontack, Hartik, and the legendary Mort of Bemil's Vane what founded the Bonebreakers. They were all gone now, those great men. Terrible killers one and all. With them dead, he commanded the Bonebreakers these last ten years. And he'd only gotten tougher with age.

The dwarf did some funny maneuver with her axe, lunging forward and twisting. The next thing Gorgorath knew, his sword was spinning away, knocked out of his hand by the dwarf's trickery.

Without pause, the dwarf lunged again. Gorgorath sidestepped the blow and pinned the dwarf's blade between his side and his arm. He punched down at the dwarf's wrist with his other hand. Now it was the dwarf's weapon that fell to the ground.

He grabbed the dwarf by the collar. He saw her reach for a dagger. Before she brought it to bear, he punched her in the face. Once and then again. The dwarf's head reeled back with each blow. Her eyes rolled back in her head. Blood spurted from her nose. Then he threw the dwarf with all his strength at the keep's wall, which stood but a few feet away. The dwarf smashed hard against the stone. She slid down, unmoving. Hopefully, the little witch was dead.

# 38

# THE DEAD FENS, OUTSIDE THE KEEP

*Year 1242, Fourth Age*
*Twelfth Year of King Tenzivel's Rule*

**O**b opened his eyes.

It took him a moment to realize that he wasn't dead. The pain clued him in. He must have passed out. For how long, he couldn't guess. Perhaps only a few moments. But maybe longer. His head was spinning and he was winded, his throat sore and bruised. Blood streamed down his brow; cut open when he hit the wall. Aside from that, he didn't think he was hurt.

The big one-eyed Lugron now fought with Red Tybor. Strong bastard to toss him like that. Ob lay there a moment more; he tried to catch his breath and get his bearings. He wasn't sure whether he could get up; his muscles all rubbery.

Then a Lugron loomed over him. A lanky, ugly thing, short for its kind. It raised an iron sword to finish him.

Ob still had his dagger in hand, how he hadn't dropped it, he had no idea. He lunged forward and slammed the dagger into the Lugron's belly. He thrust it in, hard, and twisted it.

The Lugron staggered two steps to the side, groaning and coughing. It dropped its sword and collapsed to its knees, a look of shock and horror on its face. It coughed again and again, blood pouring in waves from its mouth.

Ob pulled out the dagger and slashed it across the Lugron's throat. The bastard didn't flinch, though Ob was certain that he saw it coming. Maybe he welcomed a quick end knowing he was done for. Should have kept fighting, the coward.

The Lugron's lifeblood sprayed onto Ob and soaked the ground. Then he collapsed forward — fell right on top of Ob, pinning him beneath.

# 39

# THE HOLLOW, AZRAEL'S MANOR

*Year 801, Fourth Age*

Refisal handed Azrael an envelope. "A missive from the Lady Cassandra, Master."

Azrael looked up from his work and momentarily glanced at the envelope, its parchment rich and adorned, the script upon it expertly crafted, even his name spelled correctly. "An invitation to something. This is hardly the time for parties, given what's been going on in this town."

"Sometimes when the world is at its darkest, it's best to celebrate the light," said Refisal.

Azrael paused, thinking, then nodded his head. "Wisely said." He cut the seal, pulled out the parchment within, and perused it. Dyed pink was the paper. Perfumed. The same scent Lady Cassandra wore the night she visited his manor, only stronger. "Pennebray's birthday, to be celebrated this Thorsday, at dusk."

"Tomorrow," said Refisal. "That's quite short notice."

Azrael brought the invitation to his nose and inhaled, the slightest hint of a smile on his face.

"It seems you made an impression on Lady Cassandra," said Refisal. "Apparently, I did not, as she did not see fit to invite me. I trust that you will attend despite the late notice."

Azrael looked at the gnome, his eyes sad. "I would like to; I truly would. But the constable is outmatched by the killers. If they're to be stopped, more than likely, it falls to me to do it. If I patrol tomorrow night, I may catch the killers or throw off their plans, and thereby save someone. How could I attend a party, setting back my efforts by a day? Anyone killed tomorrow night would be on my conscience. I'll not have that. I will not rest until the killers are brought to justice."

"Have you made any progress?" said Refisal.

Azrael pointed to the detailed map of the town laid out on the tabletop before him. Every street, every building shown. "I've plotted the location of every attack in red. There's a clear pattern, as you can see. I believe that the killer resides on this block," he said pointing to one area near the center of the map, "or perhaps, this one. It is there that I will patrol tonight. Perhaps catch the killers on their way out, before they harm anyone else."

"How would you know them?"

"I have my ways. Besides, no one casually strolls about The Hollow's streets at night these days. Anyone out and about after dark is suspect. If the killers show themselves, I'll get them."

"Will you work with the constable and his marshals?"

"They'd only get in the way."

"I would—"

Azrael raised his hand in protest. "Do not ask me again, old friend. In the laboratory, we work together. But this is altogether different. When it comes to the sword, I work alone."

"But Master, there are two of them. Perhaps more."

Azrael smiled as he looked at the gnome. "Ha. Then I'll close my eyes and keep one hand behind my back to even the odds a bit. I can handle this, of that I've no doubt. Don't you worry."

# 40

# THE DEAD FENS, OUTSIDE THE KEEP

*Year 1242, Fourth Age
Twelfth Year of King Tenzivel's Rule*

Torbin Malvegil's heart pounded in his chest and his pulse throbbed at his temples when he heard the portcullis rise. The keep's entryway was inset into the wall and Malvegil and his men were around a corner, crouched behind debris, with no view of the gate (more importantly, no one inside had a view of them, which was why they were there). They didn't know who or what was coming out of that keep. Was it the squadron of Lugron that they spied the day before? Or something worse?

Red Tybor crouched on Malvegil's left, all his energy gathered, his muscles poised to charge. Master Gorlick knelt protectively to Malvegil's right; his face, sickly pale and glistening with sweat; his eyes, dull. Malvegil feared this was the weapon master's last battle; he didn't want to lose him — a good friend of many years, and his strong right arm. But if he were to die that day, Malvegil hoped he'd die in the battle. That was the right way for a warrior like Gorlick to go. When his time came, Malvegil wanted to go that way too. Or else, die peacefully from extreme old age, surrounded by his beloved family.

Not many Malvegils managed that.

He didn't expect he'd be one of the few.

The Lugron marched into view. It was the same crew from the previous day, only more of them. More than twice as many!

Ob immediately grabbed the Lugrons' attention, just as planned, so they were as yet oblivious of their presence. The Lugron marched in tight rows, in formation, like a military unit, and all geared up as if they expected a fight. They wore uniforms, or some semblance thereof: tabards emblazoned with their sigil — a white skull, cracked asunder on a bias, shattered bones beneath it, all on a field of blood red.

Mercenaries.

Trained killers.

Malvegil had hoped they were wayward tribesmen or even a group of marauders. If so, they'd be undisciplined, reckless, and likely cowardly. Easy prey for the Lomerians, despite their greater numbers. But mercenaries would be a challenge. They'd be tough. This was going to be a fight. And they were outnumbered at least five or six to one. Bad odds. Very bad.

Ob lured the Lugron out farther, shouting something that Malvegil couldn't quite make out. He'd give the order to charge just as soon as the Lugron were a bit farther from the gate, or when they were spotted, whichever came first.

Gabriel's hand gripped his shoulder from behind. "Now," he said. "Let's move!"

Red Tybor vaulted forward, spear in hand. Malvegil stood, as much in protest to Gabriel's order as in adherence to it. The others charged and swept Malvegil along with them. "Damn," muttered Malvegil. *Who is he to give the order? And why the heck did anyone heed him?*

Red Tybor crashed into the Lugron line, howling some Pictish war cry. He barreled through them before his comrades moved a handful of steps.

As one, Malvegil, Gorlick, Artol, Aradon, and McDuff crashed into the rear of the Lugron formation, or what was left of it after Red Tybor scattered them. At first, it was a massacre. The Lugron were caught by surprise, since all their attention had been affixed on Ob.

Then Par Talbon's explosion went off — a boom the like of which Malvegil had rarely heard. A crackling of electricity shot through the air. A wave of heat and pressure knocked Malvegil back several yards and took him from his feet. He didn't know what magic Talbon had thrown at them, but it had a nasty punch to it. A lot of Lugron were down, but whether stunned or dead, he didn't have time to tell.

Malvegil raised his sword high and brought it down as hard as he could on a confused Lugron's shoulder. The honed blade sliced through the man's armor, which offered it little resistance. The blade stuck fast halfway down the man's chest. Try as he might, Malvegil couldn't pull it out. The Lugron twisted, fell, and wrenched the sword from Malvegil's grasp.

A dozen or more Lugron came at Malvegil and his men. The head of a spear thrust toward Malvegil's chest. He caught the blow on his shield as he backpedaled, but he was off balance and fell backward. He landed on his rump; mud splashed up onto his face. Just to his right, he saw Gorlick slice an arm off a Lugron with one of his swords, while his second blade took off the top half of the same Lugron's head. Gorlick's injured arm didn't seem to slow him down, at least not with battle at hand.

The spearman came at Malvegil again. He rushed the Lomerian, determined to skewer him. And there sat the great lord of the Malvegils — on his butt, his sword lost, mud dripping down his face, only a shield to protect him.

A tough spot.

But Malvegil had been in worse. He'd block the next thrust and then figure something out. As the Lugron came in, Artol's hammer crashed atop its head — cracked it like an egg. Malvegil scrambled to his feet just in time to hear a roar from behind him.

He turned his head and saw a mass of Lugron, another full squadron, charge howling through the gate. Malvegil had thought he and his had ambushed the Lugron. But now, it seemed, it was the Lugron that had ambushed them.

Only one man stood between Malvegil and that murderous horde.

Sir Gabriel.

# 41

# THE DEAD FENS, OUTSIDE THE KEEP

*Year 1242, Fourth Age
Twelfth Year of King Tenzivel's Rule*

In that moment, as that squadron of Lugron came howling through the keep's gate, Malvegil expected Gabriel to go down, despite his storied skills. No man could stand alone against such a charge. No man could withstand it. No man could survive it.

But Gabriel did.

He, his sword, his shield — they were a blur of motion, too fast to follow. They bashed, sliced, thrust, and killed. The Lugron fell like cut wheat. Bodies piled about Gabriel's feet.

Deadly skills or no, the entryway was too wide, Gabriel could not block it alone. Donnelin and Karktan were nowhere to be seen. Most of the Lugron reinforcements rushed around Gabriel and toward the main melee, shouting, wide eyed, not knowing what was going on, except that battle was joined and blood was spilled. The odds were steep, even for Lomion's best.

Malvegil shouted for the others. McDuff was there at his side. So was Artol. His sword lost, Malvegil drew his Valusian dagger, a relic passed down by his ancestors for more generations than any could recall, forged of a steel alloy that even Dyvers couldn't match. The blade hardly needed honing, and though he named it a dagger, it was the length of a short sword.

Malvegil bashed his shield into an onrushing Lugron, then thrust the Valusian blade into its sternum. That antediluvian weapon pierced the Lugron's leather jerkin with almost no resistance. As the man staggered, Malvegil bashed the shield across his face, crunching bone and shearing flesh.

Malvegil saw McDuff's axe working up and down, up and down, bloody bits flying off its blade while the dwarf shouted the battle cries of his legendary clan.

Artol's hammer wreaked bloody havoc. His reach was so long, his hammer so large, his presence cleared the Lugron away and left one of Malvegil's flanks protected — so long as he stayed clear of the hammer's business end.

Despite all the Lomerians' skills, the Lugron pushed them back. Three men could not hold a dozen skilled Lugron warriors, not without giving ground and maneuvering. It put their backs to the others.

Malvegil heard Aradon behind him. The great lord of the Eotrus grunted each time he struck or parried or blocked. Malvegil pitied the Lugron that dueled with him. Even amongst Northmen, known for their size and strength, Aradon was large, his muscles matched by few men in all the realm. What it must have felt like to take one of his blows against your sword or shield. The fact that few of his opponent's still stood after he'd swung at them more than twice told all that one needed to know.

So too did Malvegil hear more of Par Talbon's magic. The great war wizard. His name whispered throughout the realm when men spoke of battle mages. A legend was he. Admired. Feared. Mysterious. His reputation outshining even that of his father, a grandmaster of the Tower of the Arcane. Most of Talbon's sorcery was subtle, but deadly. "Pop, pop, pop," went his sounds, tiny explosions set off from his hands. With each "pop", Lugron fell before him, small holes blasted in their bodies, their flesh smoking, sometimes even catching afire.

Malvegil had seen Talbon in action before, more than once. Up in the mountains. In the deep woods. Against Lugron, bandit, and marauder. Talbon killed them without emotion. He was cold that one. A man of ice. But only in battle. Elsewise, he was kind hearted, thoughtful, and as loyal as any man ever was. He'd follow his lord into Helheim and back, Talbon would, if Aradon asked it of him.

They were back to back now. Nowhere to run, nowhere to maneuver. It was victory or death. Now Malvegil not only had to keep his opponents' weapons off himself, but also had to prevent them from passing by him at all, and striking his fellows in their backs. That made the battle infinitely harder.

They could let no spear or sword thrust pass them. He saw his fellows struggling the same. In the wild melee, there was no time to watch his own back. Not even a moment to glance at what went on behind him. He had to wholly trust the men behind to guard his back. But what men they were. What heroes.

# 42

# THE HOLLOW AZRAEL'S MANOR

*Year 801, Fourth Age
Thorsday*

Azrael stared at his map, his eyes bloodshot, a mug of lukewarm coffee in hand. He'd just added six new red boxes to the clutter of precisely drawn annotations and carefully arranged tokens that covered much of the map. Each new token represented a crime scene discovered overnight or in the early morning hours.

Marple Butler knocked and stepped into the study carrying Azrael's breakfast tray, Refisal trailing behind him.

"Fourteen," said Azrael without looking up.

"Fourteen, Master?" said Refisal and Marple at the same time.

"Last night's victims," said Azrael. "Innocent townsfolk just like all the rest. Brutally murdered. Most of them killed in their homes, some still in their beds; their doors broken in — no one opened up willingly, not last night, not after all that's happened of late."

"A terrible thing, Master," said Marple.

"That many in one night is hard to fathom," said Refisal.

"Probably more lay elsewhere, undiscovered,"

said Azrael, "their bodies mutilated, desecrated like the others; their lives stolen. They're evil, these killers that plague our town. Evil, aberrant creatures devoid of conscience or mercy." Azrael's voice grew bitterer. "I don't know what pit they crawled up out of, but I shall send them screaming back down. They will pay dearly for what they've done to this community, to those good folk that they preyed upon."

Marple nodded. "The constable is fortunate to have your help, Master. Is there anything else you need at the moment?"

Azrael shook his head and Marple took his leave.

Refisal took a seat across the table from Azrael. "Did you encounter them last night?" he said.

"I saw nothing but a shadow," said Azrael. "The size of a dwarf, it was; slighter than most, just like the reports. It scurried across the alley at one murder scene and disappeared into the night."

"So it is a dwarf," said Refisal. "I'm happy to hear it isn't a gnome. My folk get blamed for far too much already. You saw how the marshal looked at me in that alley. It didn't matter to him that I'm as old as dirt and was only there to help. He was ready to accuse me, just for being short."

Azrael shook his head. "Unfortunately, so fleeting was the movement, so dark the night, I don't know what it was that I saw. It might even have been a gnome, though a tall one. But it may not have been anyone at all — maybe only a trick of light and shadow."

"You pursued?"

"It left no sign or trace," said Azrael. "No blood trail. Nothing to follow."

"Then a trick of the eyes it must have been," said Refisal. "For you can bring most anyone to heel."

"I can and that's what most concerns me. If these killers are skilled enough to escape me so easily, they may prove difficult to stop. All this," he said waving at the map, frustration on his face, "may be a waste of time."

"Worse, it may have led the constable's men astray," said Azrael. "I bumped into them over and over last night. I think they centered their patrols on me. They've given up on finding the killer on their own, I think. Ten days of searching night and day, all their resources brought to bear, and yet they can't find the killers."

"The town is not that big. So they followed me, hoping that I'd uncover something."

"Why go out there alone?" said Refisal. "If the marshals are skulking about anyway, why not work with them? Safety in numbers and all that."

"I don't want the watchmen underfoot when I find the killers. When I do, I want no distractions. And I don't want to advertise my skills. It will bring us unwanted attention, and lead to more trouble. What do you hear about town?"

"The town is in a panic," said Refisal. "People are packing wagons and leaving."

"Old news," said Azrael. "That's been going on all week. Only a trickle."

"No longer," said Refisal. "Hundreds of folk are taking to the roads this morning. News of the fourteen must be out. The roads north and west are clogged, most people fleeing to the big cities, while some others are heading out deep into the countryside. The Hollow is in trouble."

Azrael went to the window and looked out. Secluded as his manor was, he couldn't see much, but what little of the road he saw was crowded with wagons and carts. "The Hollow isn't in trouble," he said. "It's dying. This town has thrived for over a hundred years, but another day or two of that," he said pointing toward the wagons on the road, "and there will be little left here but the silent, decaying husks of abandoned buildings."

"You said "killers" before," said Refisal. "Have you confirmed that it is more than one? We've suspected that there were two, almost from the start."

Azrael paused before responding. "There's at least four or five of them working together," he said.

"What? That many?" said Refisal, shock on his face. "I've heard nothing of that from the marshals. Are you certain?"

"One or two men couldn't do what I saw last night. Three groups of folk they caught on the streets. The victims must have thought there was safety in numbers. They were wrong. Necks snapped. Throats torn out. Wrists slashed, cut to the bone. Ugly scenes all. Blood everywhere. No time for the killers to lap it up, or whatever they do with it."

"But the crime scenes inside were different," said Azrael. "They broke into homes. No one was spared: not adults, not old people, not children."

"They killed children?" said Refisal.

Azrael nodded. "Drained each victim of blood; down to the last drop. They ate portions of the corpses. I don't mean they bit them here and there and left marks. I mean they tore off large chunks of flesh with their teeth. Large chunks. Like wolves or mountain lions would do. They took their time about it too. Savored the experience."

"Madness," said Refisal. "What maniacs would—"

"A religious cult," said Azrael. "It's the most likely answer. There's probably a small clutch of townsfolk that have secretly worshiped some dark god for years. Then one day, one of them, one particularly short, killed someone. Claimed it was a sacrifice to his god to cover his crime, to divorce himself of responsibility. When his victim was dead, he drained the man's blood. Maybe even drank some of it. Maybe took a nibble or two and developed a taste for human flesh. Boasted to the others in the cult about dark favors granted by their god for the killing. For the bloodletting. For the cannibalism."

"Now the whole gang is at it."

"Hard to accept, that theory is," said Refisal. "There are good folk in this town; always have been. Never heard a whisper about dark cults hereabouts or of anybody with a taste for blood. This just can't be true."

"I hope that it is true," said Azrael. "Most every word of it, just as I've described."

"Why?" said Refisal, shock on his face.

"Because it's better than the alternative."

"What alternative?"

"That it's a disease. Something like rabies, but worse. An affliction that is driving men mad and compelling them to go out and kill their fellows."

"Someone would've reported the illness," said Refisal.

"Maybe they kill their families first," said Azrael. "Or perhaps the disease only affects them at night. They might not even know that they have it, not recalling what they did the next morning, like a sleepwalker. Or else they recall everything, and choose to keep it a secret to protect themselves from the law."

"Horrid," said Refisal. "You're right, Master. Better that it be a cult. What will you do?"

"I will find them. I will kill them. And that will be the end of it. And I'm not waiting for tonight. Ready my gear. I'm going to pay the folks at this address a visit," he said, pointing to an area on the map that he had circled in red.

# 43

# THE DEAD FENS, OUTSIDE THE KEEP

*Year 1242, Fourth Age
Twelfth Year of King Tenzivel's Rule*

Red Tybor crashed through the Lugron ranks. Shock and speed were his allies; the Lugron had no time to react. The first one fell to his spear, but the weapon stuck, no time to dislodge it. Out came his axe, short-hafted but massive of blade, its tip weighted to inflict maximum damage. As the Pict charged forward, three more Lugron fell to his axe in rapid succession. A single swing for each ended their lives. The Lugron formation crumbled before him. They scattered; fear taking over. The fire in his eyes, the bronze, hairless skin, and the speed of his strikes — they shocked his opponents. Made them think him more demon than man.

The fools.

Red Tybor was accustomed to such reactions. He enjoyed them; even expected them. It made the killing easier, and that was fine with him. Battle was a messy, dangerous business. He'd take any advantage that he could get.

One precise swing; one death; repeat — again and again. That was Red Tybor's way, his style. And it always broke his opponents. The brave, the bold, the stupid. It didn't matter. After seeing the carnage he inflicted, the rest fled. Unless fear rooted them. Or they longed for death. Or they thought themselves grand. Whatever their minds, he gave them over to the reaper with equal urgency and no regrets. Such was Red Tybor.

He crashed through to their rear. No Lugron could stop him. They didn't even slow him. That's when he saw Ob flung into a wall by a giant, one-eyed Lugron. Tall as a Northman, but wider, heavier. A brute.

Blood on his face, Ob slumped against the stone wall, unmoving. Maybe dead.

A score of Lugron down, dead, and smoking all around — Par Talbon's work.

The old gnome was one of the few close friends that Red Tybor had left. He didn't want to lose him, the crotchety old drunk. A fire welled up in the Pict's heart. An old, familiar rage that threatened to wrest control of his mind and body, to make him lose himself until it had run its course, or death took him. The berserker rage, it was. An inseparable part of his psyche; the dark corner of his soul. Rooted so deep it could never be expunged. It lurked within him, within every Pict — no exception, birth to grave. Some thought it the Picts' greatest strength; others, their bane or their curse. But Red Tybor used the rage to his advantage where his fellows could not. He held it back, restrained it, and ultimately, melded it to his purposes.

This time, just as in every battle, he maintained control. He remained Red Tybor, the beast within held at bay. That was his way. That's why he could live amongst the Volsungs, while others of his kind could not. Controlled or no, he planned to rend the life from that one-eye. He'd stick its head on spear's tip and display it for all to see. And if old Ob were dead, he'd do worse to One-eye than that. Much worse.

## 44

# THE DEAD FENS, OUTSIDE THE KEEP

*Year 1242, Fourth Age
Twelfth Year of King Tenzivel's Rule*

Gorgorath turned and faced the Pict even as his brethren shrank from the savage. Gorgorath had his sword again in one hand, his barbed whip in the other. No fear on his face; only grim resolve. He'd weathered a hundred battles with varied foes, some weak and sniveling, some proud and terrible. It mattered little to him. He had no fear of Picts — those scrawny, wild men of the wastelands. He'd killed their kind before. He'd roasted them on spits, tough as they were; hard to get down despite the burning hunger of deep winter when all other food was gone. He'd kill this one too, no matter his skill or resolve.

No man could defeat Gorgorath the Bonebreaker.

# 45

# THE HOLLOW, AZRAEL'S MANOR

*Year 801, Fourth Age*

Such a beautiful day, thought Azrael as he waited on the manor's porch for Refisal to fetch his gear. Sunny, warm. Everything seemed normal. So peaceful. His manor, as quiet as ever. Why couldn't he just sit there on the porch and relax in his rocking chair for the rest of the day? Give his old bones a bit of rest while he sucked in the clean country air and savored a cool drink. Couldn't he just enjoy being alive for once? He hadn't spent near as many days doing that as most men had, though he'd seen many more days go by.

Relaxing, enjoying things, being content — that was not Azrael's lot in life. Never was. There was always something to keep him from common, leisurely pursuits. Usually it was his experiments. The grand search for the cure to the plague — it had consumed his attention for years beyond count.

All that was over now.

He'd found the cure.

He should be joyous, shouldn't he? He should be jumping up and down, screaming his triumph to the heavens.

But he wasn't.

Mind you, he was happy to have finally discovered the cure. How could he not be?

But joyous?

No.

Not at all. And not relieved. He still felt a weight hanging over him.

In his bones, he knew his work was not yet done. Something nagged at him. Uncertainty. A bit of paranoia, mayhap.

Something was going to go wrong with the treatment.

He knew it.

He knew it with just as much certainty as he knew he wouldn't spend the day dozing on the porch. The serum was going to have side effects. The odds of it not, were just too small. The question was, how serious would the side effects be? Would the cure prove to be only temporary — their ailments to return with a vengeance? Would the serum cause some other, seemingly unrelated harm to the patients? Worse, would it kill them — some slow, agonizing death, undeserved by any? He didn't know. He didn't have any way to find out. Save for time and patience. Wait and see. Check in on the patients, monitor their conditions, and treat whatever needed treating as best he could. That was all he could do.

The waiting was difficult. That was a strange notion for a man that had lived so long and endured so much, for a man that felt years pass as others felt a single afternoon.

Yet one month, four brief weeks, seemed now an eternity. One week of that month remained before he'd release the cure to the world.

One week.

Not very long at all. Yet he knew that he'd never get there. That something bad was going to happen regarding the cure.

He hated himself for thinking that.

And he couldn't even pass that one month in peace.

Now he had to stop a group of madmen, probably religious zealots. People capable of the vilest crimes imaginable.

Azrael could not rest while there were wrongs to right. People to save. Killers to bring to justice. He had to do it. He hoped that the buildings he'd zeroed in on housed a secret temple. That he'd catch the cultists unaware and be done with them. He wanted it over with. The Hollow didn't deserve such suffering.

Then the thought popped into his head that if he saw his business done that day, perhaps he could attend the birthday celebration of dear Pennebray that evening.

With the killers brought to justice, it truly would be a celebration. A joyous one to be remembered. And he'd be a hero again. Just as he had been in olden days.

Beloved.

Appreciated.

Honored.

It had been too long. Too long that he'd lived in obscurity. Too long since he'd made a difference in the world. Too long, just being a common man, or rather, pretending to be. He was more than that. And he always would be, until the day he died, if such a day were ever to come.

On the chance that he'd be successful, he picked up the party invitation to check the address. He knew that Lady Cassandra and her daughter were still staying with her sister, but he had no idea where their villa was. He hoped that it was well away from the center of town. For there, later that day, he expected a bloodbath.

Azrael's eyes near popped from his head when he saw the address. He took a breath, then another, then a third, before he checked his map, unfolding it on the porch floor. He fought the urge to glance, to get the quick answer. He looked at the ledger of addresses, of what homes and businesses lay on which blocks. He took his time, to be certain.

There was no doubt.

There was no mistake.

The home of Lady Cassandra's sister lay at the center of the block from which the killings emanated.

Another man may have wondered, may have feared some connection, or may have been smart enough, brave enough, or bold enough to connect the dots. But even then, it would have just been a theory. Nothing more than a theory.

Azrael immediately knew.

He had a wider view than other men did. Greater perspective. More experience. He saw connections that they did not. He knew exactly what it meant.

How could the possibility have failed to cross his mind before?

How could he have missed it?

So happy was he that he had found the cure.

It had blinded him.

But now he knew.

And he knew what he had to do. And he knew what they planned for him at that party. It was the only way that they could get him. His house was too secure. The walls too high, too thick. His House guard, trusted and loyal, capable and tough, and never on their own.

They could have jumped him in the night, during his patrols, but they didn't know he was out there. Just an alchemist they thought him. Maybe a hedge wizard, nothing more.

They didn't know who he really was. They had no idea of what he was capable. That was his singular advantage.

He would put an end to the madness that night.

\*\*\*

"**M**aster—"

"No," said Azrael. "For the last time, you can't come with me. If I'm right, this will be a bloodbath. That's no place for an old man. You will await me here. I'll leave two guards with you and the servants. All doors and windows to remain locked until my return or until daybreak tomorrow."

"If I don't return, pack up your things and supplies and get well clear of the town by noon tomorrow. Continue on at your best pace until nightfall, and longer, if the moons allow. Do not return to The Hollow. Warn the Order of the

Arcane. They'll figure out what to do."

Azrael walked to House Falstad Villa, two guardsmen by his side. Six more followed at a distance, just barely keeping him in sight. He'd given them all orders to wait outside, watching the front entrance and back, awaiting any sight or sound of trouble within. Upon so sensing, they were to burst in and come to Azrael's aid, as best they could.

# 46

# THE DEAD FENS, OUTSIDE THE KEEP

*Year 1242, Fourth Age
Twelfth Year of King Tenzivel's Rule*

**R**ed Tybor's gaze — the wild eyes of a savage born and bred in the barren lands of the far northwest — bore into the one-eyed Lugron. As the Pict charged, Gorgorath launched the barbed end of his whip at his face. Red Tybor ducked it; his speed uncanny. He raised his war axe to cleave Gorgorath asunder. But the old Lugron was quick too. He dropped his whip; he swung his sword (a prize pirated from the captain of a plundered vessel) in an overhand arc. He timed it perfectly.

The two blades met with the full strength of their masters behind them — the stolen steel sword of the primitive crashed against the polished steel of the savage.

An equal match.

The explosive crack as they met and shattered rocked the battlefield.

Each man staggered back, their eyes wide, shocked and angered at the loss of their prized weapons; their hands at once numbed and stinging, their arm muscles throbbing.

Each pulled a long dagger from their belts. Red Tybor rushed in and the two veterans exchanged slash for slash, punch for punch, kick for kick. Gorgorath was the larger, the stronger, and an expert with both dagger and fists, but Red Tybor was the swifter and the more precise.

Opponents expected the Pict's blows to be wild and undisciplined, a match to his people's reputation, but Red Tybor's strikes were the opposite. Every movement he made was precise and measured; no wasted energy, no missed opportunity.

Gorgorath employed quick, powerful strokes designed to destroy a man with a single blow, despite his modest weapon. Unlike the Lugron, without his axe, Red Tybor adapted his style. Upended it. With a smaller, lighter weapon in hand, now he danced in and out. He dodged. And he struck. But only when he saw an opening.

And saw one, he did.

The Pict's dagger flashed by. It opened an ugly wound in Gorgorath's forearm, blood spouting. Another slash opened the side of the Lugron's face. It cut through his cheek to the bone — the Lugron's missing eye hampering his defense. Many warriors, perhaps most would have been out of the fight at that point, but not Gorgorath. He ignored his wounds and counterattacked.

The Lugron scored a powerful punch to Red Tybor's jaw. The Pict reeled backwards but recovered immediately. As Gorgorath plowed forward to press his advantage, Red Tybor sidestepped and landed a vicious cut to Gorgorath's thigh that made him howl.

They traded blow for blow, droplets of sweat flying from their bodies, the stench of burned flesh filling their nostrils.

As the duel wore on, Gorgorath fought mechanically, relying on instinct and power, dispensing with tactics and any remnant of finesse. He never faced an opponent that was so fast. That was so skilled. He felt the Pict's dagger slice him once, and then again, both times to the forearm, one blow cutting deep. He ignored it.

He couldn't get through the Pict's defenses. The bastard blocked every blow. He kicked at him, but the savage sidestepped it. He punched, but the Pict dodged. He slashed, but then the Pict was behind him, slicing through his armor, cutting deep into his back.

Gorgorath roared and thundered; he slashed and sliced; he stabbed, stomped, and whirled, but his blows, for all his skill, for all his experience, did him no good. Just like Old Mog, he was outmatched.

The Pict dodged or parried every strike, countered every punch, even as he opened more gashes about Gorgorath's body, calf to forehead. The blood streamed down from a head wound into Gorgorath's eyes. It stung, and made him blink — harder and harder to see. But he kept fighting. He wouldn't give up. He wouldn't lose. Not to a Pict, no matter how skilled.

Not to anyone.

# 47

# THE DEAD FENS, OUTSIDE THE KEEP

*Year 1242, Fourth Age
Twelfth Year of King Tenzivel's Rule*

Red Tybor bided his time. He was patient. He feinted and dodged and kept a wary eye toward other Lugron that might stand against him. He let the one-eyed Lugron bleed; every drop of his blood that spilled weakened him, even as the roar and chaos of battle raged around them.

The Lugron began to slow. His face went sickly pale. It was time to finish him; there was more killing yet to do. That's when Red Tybor lunged in. He blocked Gorgorath's desperate cut, grabbed his arm, and buried his blade to the hilt in the Lugron's sternum. So powerful was that strike, that the blade sliced through Gorgorath's chainmail and leather cuirass. The Pict angled the blow upward. Into the Lugron's heart.

Gorgorath saw the blade coming. He tried, but he couldn't move fast enough to block it.

The blade sank deep into his chest at an upward arc. He had been stabbed scores of times, but never like that.

Never a mortal blow.

It didn't hurt as much as he expected it would.

But he knew he was done for. He knew that the Bonebreakers had met their match. He knew that they were finished.

His strength sapped, as he fell to his knees, his eyes darted this way and that, looking for his son.

He saw him.

And in that last moment of life, he was happy.

**B**efore Red Tybor turned to seek his next opponent, a huge mallet crashed into his back. He was blasted forward and landed on his knees, ribs shattered, all air driven from his lungs.

# 48

## THE HOLLOW, FALSTAD MANOR

*Year 801, Fourth Age*

"Thank you so much for coming, your wizardship," said Lady Dahlia to Azrael, her black, ornamental party mask bounded by flaming red hair that flowed about her face and shoulders and far down her back. The mask, which covered the area around her eyes and cheeks, prevented Azrael from discerning how closely her face resembled that of her sister, Cassandra (Pennebray's mother), but there was no hiding the difference in their figures. Where Cassandra was of modest height and slim, Dahlia was tall and curvaceous, and judging by her dress, was more than comfortable putting those curves on display. Exactly the kind of woman that caught Azrael's attention, but also made him nervous. Not to say other kinds of women didn't make him nervous. It was a matter of degrees.

"As you can see," said Lady Dahlia, "My dear niece is fully recovered from her illness, thanks to you. Our family will be forever in your debt."

Pennebray stood at her side, a shy smile on her face, her straight, blonde locks reaching down to her knees. Lady Dahlia gently tapped the girl's back, prompting her to speak.

Pennebray smiled and handed Azrael a red party mask. "Thank you for making me better, your wizardship."

"You're most welcome," said Azrael. He looked over at Lady Dahlia. "In truth, I'm only an old alchemist and tinker; I'm no wizard."

"Nonsense," said Lady Dahlia. "You are much too modest and certainly not old. Wizards command powers over life and death; they control forces beyond the understanding of common folk. That is the very essence of a wizard. Only via the skilled use of such powers did you save Penny — and several others about town, if the rumors be true. You, sir, are a wizard whether you care for the title or not. And we honor you for your service."

Azrael bowed his head respectfully.

"What I don't understand," said Lady Dahlia, "is why I haven't met you before. I thought we Falstads knew everyone in The Hollow."

"I don't get out much," said Azrael.

"Well, perhaps we will have to change that," said Lady Dahlia.

Azrael felt his face flush and turned away to look at Pennebray. "Have you experienced any problems, pains, anything out of the ordinary? Anything at all?"

Pennebray shook her head. "I feel great; better than ever."

"I'm glad to hear that," said Azrael, an honest smile on his facv cm e. "I don't see your mother about."

"My dear sister, the duchess, is momentarily

indisposed," said Lady Dahlia. "Fixing her hair, no doubt. Never fear, she'll join us shortly." She gripped Azrael's arm and leaned in close, her words only for him. "Truth be told, my sister is a bit smitten with you, wizard."

"Is she?" said Azrael doing his best to hold back a smile. He had hoped as much.

"She is. Can't stop chatting about you. Day and night, it's Azrael this and Azrael that. It's been quite embarrassing actually. But seeing you in person, I begin to understand her behavior," she said, her eyes locked on his. "Though I will admit that I'm quite surprised. After her marriage to that old fart, Baltan Farthing, I figured her standards wouldn't be very high — not that they ever were of course, but being married to a man as old as your father must take its toll on one's self respect, if nothing else, don't you think?"

"Arranged, was it?" said Azrael.

"My father's doing, of course," said Lady Dahlia. "Otherwise, Cassie would never have agreed. Old money are the Farthings despite being from the back woods of nowhere. That and the title were too much for my father to resist. They're both gone now, my father and Baltan. We rule the roost. Me here at House Falstad and Cassie at House Farthing."

"So there is no Lord Falstad, if I may ask?"

Lady Dahlia smiled. "I've yet to meet a man who could tame me."

She touched Azrael's arm. "If my big sister isn't quick enough, I may decide to sink my teeth into you myself," said Lady Dahlia with a flirtatious smile.

Azrael's mouth dropped open, but no words did he have.

Other partygoers pushed forward, demanding Lady Dahlia's attention, though her eyes flicked back to Azrael more than once. Azrael, half in a daze, shuffled through the crowd into the ballroom without a further word, his face red.

# 49

# THE DEAD FENS, OUTSIDE THE KEEP

*Year 1242, Fourth Age
Twelfth Year of King Tenzivel's Rule*

Grontor, Gorgorath's son, stood behind Red Tybor, mallet in hand. The Pict lay broken before him, coughing up blood.

Grontor sprang upon the stunned warrior and grabbed him from behind. He reached under the Pict's arms and cupped his massive hands about the back of Red Tybor's neck. He pushed down with all his weight and strength even as a Lugron called Radsol viciously kicked the Pict in the face, over and again.

Red Tybor, semi-conscious and grievously wounded struggled to defend himself — to wriggle free, to release the berserker rage that simmered within him.

But he could barely move. He could barely breathe. He coughed up blood and couldn't catch his breath.

Grontor bore down on him, throwing all his weight onto the Pict's back and neck.

"I will break you!" he spat.

Red Tybor couldn't get away. The faces of his wife and mother appeared before him. They were calling him home.

A moment later, Red Tybor's neck shattered — the sound near as loud as when the weapons fractured. The Pict's body went limp and Grontor flung him to the ground.

"**W**atch my back," said Grontor to Radsol. He dropped down by his father's side; blood everywhere. Gorgorath's chest was still; it did not rise and fall with breath. Grontor knew at once that his father was dead. His captain, dead. A rage within him threatened to explode; to consume him, mind and body. He wanted to tear the mercs' flesh from their bones. He wanted to make them all suffer. To make them pay.

He turned and assessed the battle, his eyes wet. It still raged, but most of his men were down. Most were dead. Most of their opponents were up, still fighting, still killing. The battle was lost. That much was obvious. Grontor couldn't believe it, but his eyes didn't lie. The way back to the keep was blocked, but even if he could get there, there weren't enough men left within to guarantee holding it against these men. Not after the losses they'd suffered in recent weeks. It didn't seem possible. Such a small force of warriors defeated Gorgorath's Bonebreakers — the greatest Lugron mercenary company in all of Midgaard. His men were the best. Or so he had thought. These mercs were better. The Bonebreakers were finished. Their proud history at its end.

Then Grontor heard that terrible croaking sound. It was them. They were coming back. The draugar. There was only one chance left to survive this.

"We're leaving," said Grontor to those few men closest to him.

"What of the warlock?" said Tribik.

"A bunch of our boys are still inside," said Teek.

"We can't help them," said Grontor. "We'll be lucky to get clear ourselves."

"But the warlock —" said Radsol.

"To Helheim with him," said Grontor. "No amount of coin is worth dying for. Let's fly."

They skirted the edge of the battle, running flat out most of the way. Even still, the Volsungs picked off two of their number as they went. Grontor, Radsol, Teek, and Tribik made it to the far side of the skirmish, the draugar approaching from the other side of the main melee.

Grontor and his men ran and they didn't stop running until they reached the spot, a league away, where the Bonebreakers had stashed their longboats. With them, they made good their escape, and lived to fight another day.

## 50

# THE DEAD FENS, THE KEEP

*Year 1242, Fourth Age
Twelfth Year of King Tenzivel's Rule*

Gabriel hacked and slashed at the Lugron as they rushed out from the keep's gate, angry with himself, for he called for the charge too soon and got the Lomerians caught between two groups of foes.

A costly mistake, but perhaps one that there was no way to avoid. He hadn't known how many Lugron were within. He still didn't know. But he had to call for the attack while the Lugron were still unaware of their presence or else risk them retreating inside behind a locked gate that he had neither the time nor the manpower to get through.

Considering how many were spilling out of the keep, it would be a close thing, this fight. If too many of the Lugron were highly skilled, he might lose the whole expedition.

Aradon might fall.

And the line of kings with him.

Gabriel couldn't allow that. All that he fought to protect all these years might come to naught due to one pointless skirmish in the swamp gone wrong. Always a wonder, how the world turned on the smallest of things. Nor could he allow whatever monster was behind the shamblers to live. He had to stop that fiend and all the shamblers too, whatever the cost.

But protecting the line of kings was his first duty. He'd deal with the master of the Fens later.

Gabriel set to work against the Lugron, making use of sword and shield to equal skill and destructive result. He held nothing back, though he balanced attack with defense — he would do Aradon little good if he got hacked up in the battle.

Gabriel moved like lightning. For each swing of a Lugron's weapon, he swung his thrice, at least. All his blows had power and leverage behind them. All targeted vulnerable areas. He allowed no battle fury to carry him away. Every stroke was measured and balanced. Every movement planned, though not nearly to his liking.

Battle was chaos.

It was danger personified. Anyone could be hit, injured, maimed, or killed.

At any time.

Even him.

Even him.

He had to keep telling himself that.

He was not invulnerable.

No man was.

No man ever had been.

Such thoughts were never far from the forefront of his mind. Such thoughts kept him sharp. They kept him quick. They kept him from throwing caution to the wind. And thus, they kept him alive — in that battle, and all those down through the ages, through time immemorial. Back before recorded history. Back unto the Age of Heroes when he and his fellows strode across Midgaard, giants among men. When armies followed them. When nations bowed to them.

The days of glory.

And back even further. Back unto the Age of Myth and Legend. When gods walked Midgaard. And the fate of mankind was sealed by another plague.

Gabriel would not be stopped. Not by a band a Lugron mercenaries. Not by the shambling dead. Not by their master. Not by any mortal. He would not be defeated.

He had his mission. His duty. Nothing could stand in his way.

Not now.

Not ever.

The bodies of the torn dead heaped around him.

Five Lugron down

Seven.

Ten lay dead around him.

More lay dying. Their numbers thinned. The battle ebbed. But the Lugron fought on where they should have run. What kept them in the fight? What duty? What fear? Of who or what? Gabriel did not know. But he suspected that they feared the swamp and the dead things that wandered in it more than they feared Lomerian blades.

The fools.

They'd die for it. So be it.

At last, there was a break in the action. No foe stood before or behind him. Aradon was still up and fighting, apparently unscathed. The others beside him. The battle was still close. But it was theirs. He was certain of it. He vaulted for the entryway, leaping over the torn dead.

Donnelin and Karktan came up beside him dragging the wagon, just as planned. Even in the chaos of battle, they didn't shirk from their duty. Good soldiers. They were battered and bruised, their weapons bloodied. They'd done their parts.

"Get it under the gate and hold position," said Gabriel. "Don't let them drop that portcullis."

As he reached the entryway, the portcullis was headed down. Gabriel went through, searching for the mechanism that operated it, but it was nowhere in sight.

Then he heard the gate fall; the chains must have snapped, or some gear let loose. Wood splintered. Gabriel turned to see the remnants of the wagon crushed and broken, half on one side of the gate, half on the other. He was trapped inside. The others outside. Exactly what they had tried to avoid. Donnelin and Karktan had their backs to the gate and were fighting more Lugron. It was still a close thing, maybe closer than he had thought. He should've stayed outside. Aradon might still be in danger.

Another mistake.

This one he should have avoided. But the ankh pulled him inside. It influenced him in a way it rarely did. He could feel it. A tugging. A longing that he couldn't understand. It wanted him within that keep. It wanted him to find the keep's master.

And he would.

But he was on his own.

That made it harder. But he would do what need be done. Whatever need be done.

## 51

# THE HOLLOW, FALSTAD MANOR

*Year 801, Fourth Age*

**I**'m older than dirt, thought Azrael as he walked away from Lady Dahlia, into House Falstad's ballroom, but still an idiot, still a coward — with women. No excuse for it; none at all. Makes no sense, but I can't change.

After Azrael had bludgeoned himself enough, at least for the moment, he stopped staring at his feet and banished the negative thoughts from his mind.

He looked around to find himself amid a throng of revelers nearly two hundred strong, most masked in black, fewer in red. The room had a polished wood floor, and was high-ceilinged with great chandeliers of crystal. Tables lined the room's perimeter, chairs and benches on both sides. The room's center was open, save for the partygoers that milled about, chatting, laughing, and guessing at each other's identities.

As Azrael walked through the hall, he held onto the mask but chose not to put it on. It would limit his vision; he wouldn't abide that — not until he decided the place was safe.

Seeing the large crowd alleviated most of his concerns about the true nature and purpose of the party. When he had first realized that House Falstad stood at the very address at which he deduced the killer likely resided, his imagination took over. Rather than consider that someone else in the household was to blame, or someone from a nearby residence, he immediately jumped to the conclusion that it must be Pennebray, the little girl that he cured.

She was the killer.

She was the fiend!

The cannibal that had murdered goodly folk, devoured chunks of their flesh, and drained them dry of blood. She was the skinny "dwarf" that eyewitnesses had reported. Azrael's treatment had somehow driven the little girl mad, or turned her into a monster.

The other townsfolk that he'd treated must have been affected as well. They would have committed most of the murders, for the girl alone surely could never have managed them. Not to mention that many of the eyewitness descriptions of the killer told of a tall, broad man. Mikel Potter was fairly tall. So was Ebert Cook.

The very thought that that beautiful, innocent little girl might have become a craven killer — an inhuman monster — because of him, because of his actions and his alone — the unintended side effects of his so-called cure for the plague, was unimaginable.

It made his skin crawl.

It made him want to vomit.

A mad notion it was. And he knew it. There was no logical reason to jump to such a wild conclusion. It was nothing but his paranoia — that disease of the mind that had long afflicted him. An old enemy that always lay in wait, lurking about, ready to confound and cripple him. And that was just one of his failings.

But still, paranoia aside, the geographic pattern of the killings, the location of House Falstad's Manor — it couldn't be a coincidence. Could it? There had to be a connection. It nagged at Azrael. There were too many questions unanswered. And a killer or killers still to find and to bring to justice — no matter whom he, she, or they turned out to be.

When the thought first crossed his mind that Pennebray was the killer, he had been so certain of it.

Certain.

How foolish he felt as he stood there in the big hall amongst the cheerful crowd, soft music of harp and lute playing in the background. A merry occasion. A celebration of life, youth, and health. And of hope for the future. A needed diversion from the horrors that had beset The Hollow for the past fortnight. And rather than sit back and enjoy it along with everyone else, he searched for nooses and knives at every turn and in every corner.

Azrael was never able to just live, to enjoy, to be content in the now. Always there was some dark shadow hanging over his thoughts, some harbinger of doom ready to turn his world upside down. It was no way to live. But it was all he knew. He was too old to change. He made the best of it, as he always did, and soldiered on. That was his way.

Azrael looked back at the entry. Pennebray still stood by her aunt, pale but lovely in a bright pink dress, giggling and joking with those arriving as she greeted them. She was one of the few that wore no mask, as was tradition, since the party was in her honor.

Very few of the other partygoers could Azrael identify. The mayor was there, his girth, unmistakable, despite the party mask; his wife even larger; hopefully, their bench was sturdy. The constable sat next to them — full dress uniform, clean and crisp. Azrael didn't like the man; he hadn't from the first. Several marshals and their wives sat around them. Even they needed a night off from the hunt for the killer. Such things drain a man. Sometimes you have to go back to living a little, enjoying life, if even for only a brief time, to recharge, to get perspective.

Azrael wondered how many other prominent citizens of The Hollow were hidden behind the masks. He suspected that it was more than a few. Apparently, Pennebray's party was the social event of the season.

Had Azrael known that, he would have stayed home.

He didn't care for crowds and had little skill or patience for small talk.

In his paranoia, until he arrived, Azrael had imagined that the entire party was a trap for him. That Pennebray, or whoever the killer or killers were, lured him there to make him their next victim. Kill the wizard and eat his guts, maybe absorb some of his powers. The crazies always seemed to think such things. He half expected to find the manor deserted, the killers lurking in hiding, waiting to pounce on him if he stepped through the door.

He knew he was wrong the moment the servants opened the outer door at his knock — he heard the crowd within, and smelled the scent of a feast. How embarrassed he felt.

He'd shared his concerns about the party not only with Refisal, but with his guardsmen too. The old gnome didn't care. He was loyal. He knew his master's quirks and failings. He'd think no less of him over this.

But the guards were a different story. They waited outside for him, probably laughing. Their wacky old master, the mad wizard, the crazed hermit, off making a fool of himself again.

Hopefully they wouldn't quit.

Hopefully, for them, they'd dare not poke fun at him over it. Azrael didn't like being made the fool. He didn't often anger, but that was something that angered him.

He had no love of parties or crowds of any kind, did Azrael. Being a hermit was better; more comfortable. Getting lost in his work, in his search for the cure — that was his element. That was where he belonged. Where he was at his best.

In a ballroom, he felt like a fish out of water. He imagined that most of the eyes in the room were on him. He didn't like that; not one bit. He didn't like being the center of attention — or even at its far edge.

Despite his better judgment, he put on his mask. The thing covered up a good chunk of his face. A bit of armor to keep the prying eyes off him. He relaxed almost immediately. At least now some folks wouldn't know it was him.

Of course, he couldn't hide the fact that he was taller than anyone else in the room. Once he sat down that wouldn't give him away, especially if he slouched. Maybe then they'd stop staring; they'd leave him alone. That's all he wanted after all. To be left alone. To have a quiet, solitary life, so he could finish his work, and in so doing, help people — and atone for his past transgressions. He could do that the better, a lot better, if everyone just left him alone.

He hoped that there wouldn't be dancing. Thank goodness for the mask. Maybe they'd leave him alone, the women that were there. If not, he'd make good his escape, somehow. It didn't seem likely he'd find any killers there that night, so he could leave whenever he felt the need. And he was beginning to feel it.

# 52

# THE DEAD FENS, THE KEEP

*Year 1242, Fourth Age*
*Twelfth Year of King Tenzivel's Rule*

**B**eyond the portcullis, in front of Gabriel, was a long hall, more tunnel than corridor, the low ceiling arched in the same stone as the walls and floor. It stood empty of Lugron. Perhaps all that there were, were already outside. The floor was wet, cracked, and sloped downward as he went. Ten steps in and the water was over the toes of his boots and grew deeper by the step. By the time he reached the end of the corridor, it was past his knees. All muddy, completely opaque, and with a stink that was part sewer, part charnel house. It made the bog smell like a meadow.

Every sound Gabriel made echoed throughout the place, his path lit by torches set in wall sconces along the way. Cobwebs hovered above his head in a thick white mesh, but thankfully, tall as he was, he could walk upright without getting webbed in the face, though barely.

He saw the slight ripple in the water as he reached the corridor's end. He knew Lugron stood around the bend, waiting in ambush. How many? He didn't know, except that there weren't so many that they were brave enough to come out and charge him.

That meant that there weren't enough. Not enough to stop him.

He threw some flotsam against the far wall in hopes of drawing them out. A big axe cleaved through the air just where he would have been if he had walked around the corner, and an even bigger Lugron lumbered into view, grunting in frustration at his wasted swing. The man must have weighed five hundred pounds, his leather jerkin bursting at the seams as it tried to constrain his bulk.

Gabriel thrust his sword into the side of the Lugron's chest. The man opened his mouth and let out a growl as his knees buckled and he dropped to them, his face full of shock. Then Gabriel took off the Lugron's head with a single, powerful swing. He did that more for effect than anything else — for the man was out of action and would have died shortly anyway. Gabriel wanted to scare the others. To shock them. To freeze them in their tracks.

It worked perfectly. Even as he completed his headshot, he stepped around the corner, hugging the wall, so that the big Lugron was still in clear sight of his fellows. Three others stood there, their mouths open, their feet rooted in place as they saw the big man fall.

Two lightning thrusts with his blade sent the nearest two to the afterlife. The third backpedaled two steps as his friends fell, then turned, and ran for it, splashing through the water, shouting for help. Gabriel could have thrown a dagger at him, and probably dropped him, but he decided not to bother. They'd be expecting him now. They'd be ready. But they'd also be afraid. He'd use that fear to his advantage in every way that he could. One man alone against many had to do that in order to survive.

Morbid though it was, Gabriel picked up the big Lugron's head and carried it by the hair. Seeing him holding that would put the fear in the other Lugron. And fear was a weapon. A weapon that was sometimes far more effective than a sword. Azathoth had taught Gabriel that, long ago. A lesson he had never forgotten.

Gabriel followed after the fleeing Lugron, but he did so slowly, cautiously, for the place was large, dark, and dangerous. Any number of Lugron or worse might lie within. He was wary of ambushes, traps, and pits in the floor that he couldn't see until he stepped into one. It bordered on reckless to move through such a place alone with enemies about. And Gabriel was not a reckless man, not then or ever, but he had little choice but to continue.

He watched for movement in the water, listened for any sound, kept his eyes peeled for traps. There were big rooms on either side of the corridor, their doors long gone, rotted mayhap, or else used for firewood or for reinforcing the main doors. The rooms stood barren and as flooded as was the main corridor. Gabriel saw no one within, but there were dark corners and depths to those chambers that could have hidden many foes. He had no time to search them, and he didn't want to stray off the main path or else risk entrapment in some windowless chamber. Most of the rooms looked as if they'd been deserted for a long time. The castle looked dead. But nothing in Lomion was as it appeared.

The sounds of the battle outside dimmed as he ventured farther into the keep's depths, but after a short time, they grew louder again. Perhaps there were windows nearby that overlooked the battle, though he didn't see any, or mayhap the Lugron had rallied or more of their number had showed up, increasing the racket. It mattered not. He could not aid his friends now. He had to trust to their skills. It fell to him alone to find the source of the shamblers, the master of that place. He would see it dead.

He heard sounds from up ahead. The runner reporting to his friends. Gabriel proceeded as silently as he could, gliding through the water. He bypassed several chambers and numerous narrow, steep flights of stone steps that likely led up to arrow slit positions or murder holes. Soon he came upon a broad stone stair that led upward, curving in a wide arc as it hugged a rounded wall, no doubt the turret of the main tower. The steps emerged from the muddy water and went up some twenty feet to an upper level. Atop the stair, the Lugron awaited him. A squad of them: spearmen, swordsmen. Six or eight at the least. Maybe more behind. A wall of spears and shields that stretched across the stair. Their final line of defense? He hoped so.

"Put down your weapons if you want to live," said Gabriel.

They answered him with a spear. A well placed throw. Would have hit his breastplate, if not for his shieldwork. It bounced off the spiked metal plate in the center of his shield and clattered to the floor.

"Last chance," said Gabriel. "Give up now or we will cut out your eyes and feed them to our dogs." Another spear was their answer. And that was fine with Gabriel. He wanted them to loose those spears now, at a distance, when he could easily block them.

They refused to accommodate him further, answering his taunts only with expletives. Four voices.

He should have stayed outside with the others. Fighting his way through the keep on his own was foolish. He risked himself. He risked the line of kings. And for what? He didn't even know. Nothing was worth that. Yet he had to go on. Something drew him in. The ankh for certain, but something more. Something compelled him forward.

The hand of fate?

He didn't believe in such foolishness. Not anymore. Not for a long time. Yet some beliefs, some notions, however foolish, were hard to let completely go of.

He walked up the steps. He could barely see the Lugron behind their spears and their armor. Eyes and not much else. Even that was tough in the darkness.

They'd thrown torches down on the steps, the better to see him coming, while they stood hidden in shadow. That was stupid.

Gabriel sheathed his sword and picked up the torches, one, two, and the third, stretching his grip to the limit to carry them all, and the Lugron's head, in his sword hand as he held his shield up protectively with the other. He walked slowly up the stairs, the Lugron murmuring and shifting as he came. They were nervous. They were scared.

They should be. He only made out fragments of what they said to each other.

"Only one Volsung," they said.

"He's alone," they said.

By the time he was halfway up the steps, and with no support in sight, the Lugron grew confident. They argued amongst themselves as to who would get his sword, his shield, his armor.

Stupid.

Gabriel liked stupid opponents. All the easier to defeat. If he wanted a challenge, he'd play Mages and Monsters against Aradon and Talbon. This melee would be no challenge.

Gabriel tossed the dead Lugron's head up at them. It landed in their midst to a chorus of gasps and curses.

"What was his name?" said Gabriel. "What was his name!"

"Mordo," said a shaky voice.

"A big man was Mordo," said Gabriel. "His flesh was tasty, though we had no time to chew him to the bone. But we'll take our time with you."

That set them to murmuring and shifting. Some were ready to run. Gabriel kept ascending the stairs. Two thirds of the way up, he lobbed one of the torches just over the heads of the foremost Lugron. He grabbed the second torch and tossed it at their front line. He did the same with the third. The Lugron howled and parted, beginning to panic as flames danced around them.

"I will eat you to the bone," shouted Gabriel. Then he charged, his sword in his hand in an instant.

He blocked a clumsy spear thrust, and pushed another spear aside. His sword's tip found an opening between their shields and sank deep into the face of one Lugron. Another quick thrust took a second Lugron in the neck.

Their line broke and all was chaos. One Lugron went flying down the steps. Two others ran. Two more made a stand. One was skilled. Very skilled. It took Gabriel five or six swings of his sword to knock down his defenses, another three swings to kill him. The man fought to the end. A true warrior.

Gabriel hated killing men like that. And for what? What was this confrontation all about?

For silver?

They were mercenaries after all. Gabriel believed that the force behind the kidnappings, behind the shamblers, had hired these Lugron to do his bidding. That much was obvious. Now they paid the price.

# 53

# THE DEAD FENS, OUTSIDE THE KEEP

*Year 1242, Fourth Age
Twelfth Year of King Tenzivel's Rule*

**M**aster Gorlick, clad in plate and chainmail armor, labored more with each blow struck and parried. A veteran of a dozen campaigns, Gorlick was a swordsman with few peers in all the Kingdom of Lomion. He fought with two blades, a bastard sword of ornate style and a short wide blade called a Dyvers thraysk. His constitution was unmatched by other Malvegil men. Even slower to tire was he than Red Tybor. But that day, he slowed. That day, he tired. His throbbing arm plagued him. The pain so great that the arm felt numb from the elbow on down. Just enough feeling remained that he could grip his weapon. His head pounded too. A headache like he'd rarely had. A fever clouded his mind. He felt as if his blood boiled within his veins. He just wanted to lay down and sleep.

He ignored it, the pain. He fought on through the fatigue. All his will bent on slaying every Lugron within his reach. He would defend his lord to his last breath. And he would secure his place in Odin's great hall in Valhalla.

No fewer than six Lugron lay dead or dying about him. Several others staggered away, or cowered on the ground, missing an arm or a hand, or stabbed through their torsos. Still they came on, the Lugron did. Like madmen. Gorlick had rarely seen such battle lust in the face of superior skill. These were no common Lugron; no common mercenaries. They were amongst the toughest he'd faced.

With the dead piling up about him, Gorlick gutted one Lugron with his thraysk, then spun about and lopped off the head of another with his long blade. Perspiration flew off his brow and rained down his cheeks, his hair plastered to this head, his breathing labored, his movements no longer crisp and clean and smooth, yet still effective.

Still deadly.

Three more Lugron surrounded him. Was there no end to them? Several spinning moves and desperate thrusts later and two more were down, mortally wounded. Gorlick staggered, his vision growing cloudy, the sounds about him grew strangely muted. All his energy was spent.

The third Lugron, a massive beast nearly six and half feet tall and over four hundred pounds grabbed Gorlick from behind. One meaty forearm pressed tightly around Gorlick's throat, the other clamped down on his sword arm. With incredible strength, the Lugron wrenched the sword from Gorlick's grasp. In twenty years, no one had disarmed him.

Gorlick twisted and stamped on the Lugron's foot. He slipped from the choke hold. Lunged forward and pulled, flipping the massive Lugron over in the air to come crashing down on its back.

Gorlick lunged forward with his thraysk, but the Lugron was up in an instant, unharmed.

He thrust the blade at the Lugron's throat.

Blocked.

The Lugron's mace thundered down onto the blade. Shattered. The hilt spun to the ground; Gorlick's hand battered and bloody.

Owing to his fevered daze, Gorlick didn't see the backhand coming. It caught him on the jaw.

A blow powerful enough to fell a horse.

Stunned and dazed, Gorlick staggered back; barely kept his feet. His hand went for the dagger at his belt. The Lugron charged at him, arms wide. A fatal move for the Lugron, that should have been. But for his ailing arm, Gorlick couldn't pull his dagger quickly enough, his fingers unresponsive.

The Lugron swept him into a bear hug. A grip more powerful than any Volsung could manage. Only the muscles of a massive Lugron were so strong. Gorlick's arms were pinioned to his sides so tightly that he couldn't pull the dagger.

So tightly, he couldn't breathe.

Gorlick strained with all his might, his muscles bulging. "Odin!" he called to the heavens, yielding what air remained to him. But that brutal, primitive vice would not yield.

Gorlick headbutted the brute – once, and then again, and then a third time. The Lugron roared and cursed but it was all to no avail, save to slice open his own forehead and fill his eyes with a crimson stream of lifeblood. Blood streamed down Gorlick's cheeks, over his lips, a bit of it into his mouth. It was off — the blood. Its taste, foul, corrupted. He knew it was the wasting disease from the bite on his arm. The infection was all through him now.

Gorlick looked about in desperation, blinking the blood from his eyes, but there was no friend in sight. All were fighting for their own lives, the clash still desperate and close. No one to help him.

He never needed help before. Never wanted it. Never. And now the one time he did, no help was there to find.

It was not his place to need help, to call for it. His job was to provide help. To guard his lord. To safeguard his life, his family, his noble House. In the chaos, Gorlick knew not whether Malvegil even still lived. He'd failed his lord. He'd failed his friend. He'd failed in his duty. And for that, and not for himself, he knew despair.

He was alone. His vision dimmed again; the last of his strength ebbed; he could fight no more.

He had nothing left. His lungs burned. No breath remained even to call for aid.

He knew his time had come.

He would not march on the homeward road. But he had fought his best. A warrior's death it would be, thank the gods.

But he would not see his children grow up. His wife would have no husband. He would not see his daughters marry. He would not stand beside his son during his first battle. They'd have no father. Only fleeting memories. The little one, not even that.

Gorlick heard something above him, something he instinctively knew was important, but he could not place the sound.

A horse? But not a horse.

He looked up, his vision fading fast, but there, far above him, bathed in bright light, and descending from the clouds astride their white, winged steeds, he spied the Valkyries, the shield maidens of Odin, come to carry him home.

He closed his eyes, a smile on his face. He had earned his place. In that way at least, his life was complete. He let the darkness take him, for he knew then that he'd awake in Valhalla. He'd dine that night in Odin's hall amongst the honored dead. Forevermore to be counted amongst the worthy warriors of eternal Asgard. And with that knowledge, he was at peace.

He let go.

And so passed Master Gorlick the Bold, son of Thraydin and Bernda, Twenty Ninth Weapons Master to the Malvegils.

The huge Lugron held Gorlick fast. Its iron grip never relaxed — not even long after Gorlick had gone limp in its arms. He would not drop that great warrior, not until he was certain that he was dead.

Suddenly, Gorlick's eyes opened.

As if a madness was upon him, Gorlick's head sprang forward and he sunk his teeth into the leather collar of the Lugron's jerkin. Those teeth pulled with such force that the collar tore off, several of his teeth splintering in the process. As the Lugron squeezed the man anew with all its might, determined to crush the life from him, the sound of Gorlick's ribs cracking erupted over the din of the melee.

But Gorlick was not done. Letting the torn collar fall from his mouth he went for the Lugron's throat. He sank his teeth deep into the Lugron's flesh; biting and tearing like a wild beast.

The Lugron fell backward; blood sprayed from his severed jugular, his hands desperately trying to stem its flow.

Gorlick's head turned from his victim, blood pouring from his mouth, the Lugron's flesh dangling from his teeth. He was Master Gorlick no longer, and never would be again. Now he was a thing. A creature. A monster. A fiend. Now he was one of the shambling dead.

# 54

# THE HOLLOW, FALSTAD MANOR

*Year 801, Fourth Age*

A hand bell sounded across House Falstad's ballroom. Louder and louder still. A servant that stood next to Lady Dahlia rang it.

After a few moments, the room gave Lady Dahlia its attention. While she spoke to the crowd, the servants presented the first course: a stew of meat and vegetables, well seasoned but gamey. It tasted a bit off, though Azrael couldn't say why. One spoonful was all he managed. He wasn't a big eater, so it really didn't matter.

"Gathered together we are for the happy occasion of the eighth birthday of my beloved niece, Pennebray," said Lady Dahlia. Claps and cheers erupted from the crowd.

"In a child's life," she said, "every birthday is special, but for Penny, this one is the most special by far. For as many of you know, Penny was recently afflicted with a mysterious illness, both painful and life threatening. Only through the efforts of the wizard—"

Oh boy, here it comes.

"Lord Azrael the Great, did she recover and regain her strength. Not only has the illness fled, but Penny is stronger and healthier than ever."

"Here, here," shouted the mayor. "Well done, wizard, well done."

Many eyes turned toward Azrael, the mask notwithstanding.

He thanked the gods that he had put it on. It made the attention infinitely easier to bear. Dead gods, he hoped that she wouldn't ask him to make a speech. What if she called him out for the first dance of the evening — right in front of everyone? He was trapped.

There was general applause and remarks of praise for Azrael all around. That was nice to hear. Those seated nearest him, even patted him on the back. He resisted the urge to cringe and shirk away. He didn't like to be touched.

"Rumor has it," said Lady Dahlia, "that several other citizens have also recently been cured of their ailments by Lord Azrael. Please sir, stand, and take a bow."

He could do that. Bowing was easy enough. A moment and it would be over. No speech, thank the gods; a great relief. It had been a long time since anyone had called him Lord Azrael. He liked the sound of it; always had.

Azrael stood and bowed with a flourish. Somehow the mask made him bolder. Too bad he couldn't wear it all the time. If he did, all the more reason for people to think him odd. But then again, oddness was common enough and generally well tolerated amongst wizards. He'd hold on to the mask, just in case he decided to give it a go.

"Tell us, great wizard," said Lady Dahlia, "how did you work these miracles?"

Oh, boy. Things were headed downhill. Why couldn't she just let him be?

The room went silent as a tomb; every eye affixed on Azrael.

Azrael expected the contents of his stomach to spew forth immediately. Would the geyser be powerful enough to strike the mayor across the way? Would the force of it knock him over? Would it kill him outright? Drowned and pummeled to death by puke. A terrible way to go.

"Natural remedies of herbs and salts, mixed with the blessed water from The Hollow's own hot springs," said Azrael without missing a beat, his answer practiced, just in case. He was always prepared.

That answer seemed to satisfy.

"Please, everyone," said Lady Dahlia, "enjoy your stew. Soon, the servants will bring out the main course."

Eyes turned from Azrael and looked to their food. He'd survived it, the attention; the judging eyes; the annoying scrutiny.

Azrael's own gaze darted around the room. He wondered if it was but a momentary pause. Would the hall's attention soon return to him?

He studied the guests, the mask obscuring, to large extent, exactly where he was looking. He liked that. Another reason to wear it around town, despite any unwanted attention it garnered.

He found himself wishing the other partygoers wore no masks. He didn't like not knowing who was who. But he supposed that that was the point of the masks, the fun of it. Try as he might, he only recognized a few folk.

Then he noticed something odd.

Ebert Cook was there.

He knew it was the cook by his burly chest, thick build, and long gray hair. Ebert worked in a tavern on the far side of town. A rough place by all accounts. The food was excellent, owing to Ebert's talents, but even Azrael was loath to go there, for the clientele were all too seedy for his patience. Recent events notwithstanding, there wasn't much crime in town, but what crime there was often centered about that place.

An odd thing to invite such a man to a young girl's party. A man of a different social class. It was inconceivable that either Lady Dahlia or her sister frequented Ebert's tavern. Then what connection was there between them? More questions. But no answers.

Then Azrael spied Mikel Potter when the artisan's black mask slipped from his face while he chatted with a thin woman seated beside him. Strange, it wasn't his wife for she was rather plump. Then he realized, the thin woman was the washerwoman from Dunn Street that he had cured over a week before — the one with the bad limp and stooped back. She sat straight up, a feat impossible for her when he last saw her. It made no sense for a menial worker like her to be invited to a noble girl's birthday ball. In fact, as Azrael looked about, he realized that there was not a single other child in attendance. An odd thing indeed.

Azrael's paranoia crept from where he'd stowed it. The hair on the back of his head stood up. Dark thoughts washed over him. Fearful, frightening thoughts. He had trouble focusing; he fought to think, his mind was spinning. He felt his face flush. He began to sweat. Every fiber of his being told him that something was gravely wrong. In fact, he wanted to run for it. Were it not for the dreadful embarrassment that that would have caused, he may well have fled at that very moment.

The opportunity to flee passed all too quickly. The hall's main doors were blocked when the servants pushed a large wheeled table (which held the dinner's main course) into the room, and closed the hall's doors behind them. That was in accordance with tradition — latecomers to formal events were denied entry and all that. Odd that they set a crossbar down. That carried things a bit far, but the Falstads were formal and fancy, and Azrael was a bit out of touch with the subtleties of the modern aristocracy. The common folk were a lot easier to understand, more straightforward and such, but still, he preferred the refinement of taste and decor of the wealthy. He was more at home with that.

Azrael's eyes turned toward the other exits. One led to the kitchens, obvious enough, a second door off to the side probably led to a delivery or servant's entrance, two others to washrooms: one for men, the other for women. Two more doors led who knows where, maybe just closets, or mayhap, even a stairwell going up or down or both ways. If he had to flee, he'd head to the servant's entrance — probably his best chance to get away clean.

The main dinner course lay covered over with

a tablecloth. The dish was meant to be a surprise — another tradition. Azrael hoped that it was suckling pig or perhaps a small hog, though a side a beef would be welcome too. For Odin's sake, don't let it be lamb; Azrael never developed a taste for that.

The guests talked and laughed and enjoyed their stew, as soothing music played in the background. A good party, as far as parties go.

Save for the odd guest list.

Azrael's hand found the hilt of his sword. He needed to know it was in easy reach, just in case. His other hand confirmed that his long dagger was in its proper place, ready for deployment at a moment's notice. But what could happen in such a room with so many good folks gathered? Nothing, of course.

So why was he so worried?

He wasn't sure. But he knew that he had to be prepared. If the doors hadn't been barred, he'd be on his way out already, he was certain of it.

Lady Dahlia led Pennebray, carving knife in hand, to the center of the room, the birthday celebrant to make the first cut of the roast. No doubt, this was her first time old enough for the honor.

"May I have your attention?" said Lady Dahlia, her voice strong, commanding. She looked around and waited until everyone quieted down and directed their gaze on her. "Now of age," she said, "it falls to our beloved Penny to carve the meat. And such an occasion calls for no ordinary hunk of beef or venison. No common cut of lamb or pork or fatted fowl. It warrants something a bit exotic."

"A meal to be savored. To be remembered. I'm certain that you'll all enjoy it — it's lean, but very tender, and oh so sweet. I only hope that there's enough for everyone. Please don't be greedy." Lady Dahlia ripped the table coverings off with one quick motion. There, naked, and tied down so tightly to the top of that table that she could not move, lay Pennebray's mother, Lady Cassandra, a gag in her mouth.

Azrael couldn't believe his eyes. So shocked was he, that for a moment, just a moment, he was frozen in place as he tried to process what was happening. Gasps of surprise erupted from a few spots about House Falstad's ballroom, but shockingly, cheers erupted from all around.

Cheers.

What was that about? thought Azrael. Why do they cheer? It made no sense. Was he somehow misinterpreting what was going on?

And then, before his eyes, Pennebray's face twisted into an evil leer as she stared at her mother. It was not the expression of a little girl. Of a child. It was the look of a depraved killer.

And the merest moment after she put on that terrible face, her skin morphed to ghostly gray. Her eyes went black as pitch, no whites remained. And fangs grew from her mouth. Fangs like that of a serpent. Her upper canine teeth grew to three, perhaps four inches in length. She roughly pulled the gag from her mother's mouth. And she lifted up the carving knife.

Lady Dahlia looked on, beaming with pride and joy. She stepped up next to them, plucked the jeweled headband from her sister's forehead, and placed it on her own. "Who's the duchess now, big sister?" she shouted. "It should always have been me! Me! And now it is! Now I'm the duchess!"

"Duchess!" shouted the crowd.

**END**

# BOOKS BY GLENN G. THATER

## THE HARBINGER OF DOOM SAGA
GATEWAY TO NIFLEHEIM
THE FALLEN ANGLE
KNIGHT ETERNAL
DWELLERS OF THE DEEP
BLOOD, FIRE, AND THORN
GODS OF THE SWORD
THE SHAMBLING DEAD
MASTER OF THE DEAD
SHADOW OF DOOM
WIZARD'S TOLL
VOLUME 11+ (forthcoming)

## HARBINGER OF DOOM
(Combines *Gateway to Nifleheim* and *The Fallen Angle* into a single volume)

## THE HERO AND THE FIEND
(A novelette set in the Harbinger of Doom universe)

## THE GATEWAY
(A novella length version of *Gateway to Nifleheim*)

## THE DEMON KING OF BERGHER
(A short story set in the Harbinger of Doom universe)

# GLOSSARY

# PLACES

## The Realms
**Asgard**: legendary home of the gods
—**Bifrost**: mystical bridge between Asgard and Midgaard
—**Valhalla**: a realm of the gods where great warriors go after death
**Helheim**: one of the nine worlds; the realm of the dead
**Midgaard**: the world of man
—**Lomion**: a great kingdom of Midgaard
**Nether Realms**: realms of demons and devils
**Nine Worlds, The**: the nine worlds of creation
**Nifleheim**: the realm of the Lords of Nifleheim / Chaos Lords
**Vaeden**: paradise, lost
**Yggdrasill**: sacred tree that supports and/or connects the Nine Worlds

## Places Within The Kingdom Of Lomion

**Dallassian Hills**: large area of rocky hills; home to a large enclave of dwarves
**Dor Eotrus**: see Eotrus Demesne below
**Dor Linden**: fortress and lands ruled by House Mirtise, in the Linden Forest, southeast of Lomion City
**Dor Lomion**: fortress within Lomion City ruled by House Harringgold
**Dor Malvegil**: fortress and lands ruled by House Malvegil, southeast of Lomion City on the west bank of the Grand Hudsar River
**Doriath Forest**: woodland north of Lomion City

**Dyvers, City of**: Lomerian city known for its quality metalworking
**Farthing Heights**: town ruled by House Farthing.
**Hollow, The: a town;**
— **Ancestor Hill:** cemetary
— **Azrael's Manor**
— **House Falstad Manor**
**Kern, City of**: Lomerian city to the northeast of Lomion City.
**Kronar Mountains**: a vast mountain range that marks the northern border of the Kingdom of **Lomion**
**Lindenwood**: a forest to the south of Lomion City, within which live the Lindonaire Elves
**Lomion City**: capitol city of the Kingdom of Lomion

## Parts Foreign

**Azure Sea**: vast ocean to the south of the Lomerian continent
**Darendor**: dwarven realm of Clan Darendon
**Dead Fens, The**: mix of fen, bog, and swampland on the east bank of the Hudsar River, south of Dor Malvegil
**Evermere, The Isle of**: an island in the Azure Sea, far to the south of the Lomerian continent.
— **The Dancing Turtle**: Evermere's finest inn
**Grand Hudsar River**: south of Lomion City, it marks the eastern border of the kingdom
**Emerald River**: large river that branches off from the Hudsar at Dover
**Jutenheim**: island far to the south of the Lomerian continent (see below for more details).

**Karthune Gorge**: site of a famed battle involving the Eotrus
**Kronar Mountains**: foreboding mountain range that marks the northern border of the Kingdom of Lomion.
**R'lyeh**: a bastion for evil creatures; Sir Gabriel and Theta fought a great battle there in times past.
**Thoonbarrow**: capital city of the Svarts
**Trachen Marches**: Theta and Dolan fought the Vhen there.
**Tragoss Mor**: large city far to the south of Lomion, at the mouth of the Hudsar River where it meets the Azure Sea. Ruled by Thothian Monks.

## PEOPLE

### Peoples of Midgaard
**Emerald elves**
**Lindonaire elves** (from Linden Forest)
**Doriath elves** (`dor-i`-ath') (from Doriath Forest)
**Dallassian dwarves** (doll-ass`-ian) (from the Dallassian Hills). Typically four feet tall, plus or minus one foot.
**Gnomes** (northern and southern), typically three feet tall, plus or minus one foot.
**Humans/Men**: generic term for people. (In usage, usually includes gnomes, dwarves, and elves)
**Lugron** (usually pronounced 'lou-gron'; sometimes, 'lug`-ron'): a barbaric people from the northern mountains, on average, shorter and stockier than Volsungs, and with higher voices.

**Picts:** a barbarian people
**Stowron** (usually pronounced 'stow`-ron'): pale, stooped people of feeble vision who've dwell in lightless caverns beneath the Kronar Mountains
**Svarts** (black elves), gray skin, large eyes, spindly limbs, three feet tall or so.
**Vanyar Elves**: legendary elven people
**Volsungs:** a generic term for the primary people/tribes populating the Kingdom of Lomion

**House Alder** (Pronounced All-der)
A leading, noble family of Lomion City. Their principal manor house is within the city's borders
**Barusa Alder, Lord**: Chancellor of Lomion, eldest son of Mother Alder.
**Mother Alder**: matriarch of the House; an Archseer of the Orchallian Order
**Rom Alder**: brother of Mother Alder

**House Eotrus** (pronounced Eee-oh-tro`-sss)
The Eotrus rule the fortress of Dor Eotrus, the Outer Dor (a town outside the fortress walls) and the surrounding lands for many leagues.
**Aradon Eotrus, Lord**: Patriarch of the House (presumed dead)
**Claradon Eotrus, Brother**: (Clara-don) eldest son of Aradon, Caradonian Knight; Patriarch of the House; Lord of Dor Eotrus
**Donnelin, Brother**: House Cleric for the Eotrus (presumed dead)
**Ector Eotrus, Sir**: Third son of Aradon
**Eleanor Malvegil Eotrus**: (deceased) Wife of Aradon Eotrus; sister of Torbin Malvegil.
**Gabriel Garn, Sir**: House Weapons Master

(presumed dead, body possessed by Korrgonn)
**Jude Eotrus, Sir:** Second son of Aradon (prisoner of the Shadow League)
Knights & Soldiers of the House:
  — **Sergeant Artol**: 7 foot tall veteran warrior.
  — **Sir Paldor Cragsmere**: a young knight; formerly, Sir Gabriel's squire
  — **Sir Glimador Malvegil**: son of Lord Torbin Malvegil; can throw spells
  — **Sir Indigo Eldsroth**: handsome, heavily muscled, and exceptionally tall knight
  — **Sir Kelbor**
  — **Sir Ganton**: called "the bull" or "bull"
  — **Sir Trelman**
  — **Sir Marzdan** (captain of the gate, deceased)
  — **Sir Sarbek du Martegran** (acting Castellan of Dor Eotrus), a knight captain of the Odion Knights
**Malcolm Eotrus**: Fourth son of Aradon
**Nardon, Eotrus, Lord:** Aradon's father
**Ob A. Faz III**: (Ahb A. Fahzz) Castellan and Master Scout of Dor Eotrus; a gnome
**Pellan, Captain** (aka, the beardless dwarf)
**Pontly:** former Castellan of the House prior to Ob being appointed to that position
**Stern of Doriath**: Master Ranger for the Eotrus (presumed dead)
**Talbon of Montrose, Par**: Former House Wizard for the Eotrus (presumed dead), son of Grandmaster (Par) Mardack
**Tanch Trinagal, Par**: (Trin-ah-ghaal) of the Blue Tower; Son of Sinch; House Wizard for the Eotrus. Aliases: Par Sinch; Par Sinch Malaban.
**Sverdes, Leren**: House physician and alchemist

## House Malvegil
**Torbin Malvegil, Lord**: Patriarch of the House; Lord of Dor Malvegil.
**Landolyn, Lady**: of House Adonael; Torbin's consort. Of part elven blood.
**Eleanor Malvegil Eotrus**: (deceased) Wife of Aradon Eotrus; sister of Torbin Malvegil.
**Gedrun, Captain**: a knight commander in service to Lord Malvegil
**Glimador Malvegil, Sir**: son of Torbin and Landolyn; working in the service of House Eotrus.
**Gorlick the Bold, Master**: House Weapons Master – 29th Weapons Master to the Malvegils; son of Thraydin and Bernda
**Gravemare, Hubert**: Castellan of Dor Malvegil
**Hogart**: harbormaster of Dor Malvegil's port.
**Karktan of Rivenwood, Master**: Weapons Master for the Malvegils
**Mordel**: former Castellan of Dor Malvegil
**Rorbit, Par**: House Wizard to the Malvegils
**Stoub of Rivenwood**: Lord Malvegil's chief bodyguard; brother of Karktan (deceased)
**Tage, Leren:** House physician
**Torgrist, Brother**: Dor Malvegil's high cleric.
**Troopers Bern, Brant, Conger**: Malvegillian soldiers
**Tybor, Red**: House Master Scout; a Pict

## Great Beasts, Monsters, Creatures, Animals

**Blood Lord**: legendary fiends that drink blood and eat humans.
**Duergar**: mythical undead creatures
**Draugar**: undead creatures that feast on the

living
**Dwellers of the Deep**: worshippers of Dagon; huge, bipedal fishlike creatures
**Jotnar**: giants (plural of Jotun)
**Jotun**: a giant
**Ogres**:
**Leviathan**: a huge sea creature
**Saber-cat**: saber toothed tiger
**Shamblers:**
**Trolls, Mountain**: mythical creatures of the high mountains
**Wendigo**: monster of legend that eats people.

## Bonebreakers, The
Famed Lugron mercenary company
**Brontack:** former leader of the Bonebreakers (deceased)
**Gorgorath the Bonebreaker:** Captain of the Bonebreakers
**Grontor**: son of Gorgorath
**Hartick**: former leader of the Bonebreakers (deceased)
**Mog, Old**: the Bonebreaker's battle mage
**Mordo**: 500 lb Lugron soldier
**Mort of Bemil's Vane**: founder of the Bonebreakers (deceased)
**Radsol**: a Lugron soldier
**Teek:** a Lugron soldier
**Trench, Old**: the Bonebreaker's cook
**Tribek**: a Lugron soldier
**Wolfrick**: the leader of rival Lugron mercenary company

## Militant and Mystic Orders
**Churchmen**: a generic term for the diverse group of priests and knights of various orders.
**Grontor's Bonebreakers**: a mercenary company. The Lugron, Teek and Tribik belonged to it.
**Myrdonians:** Royal Lomerian Knights
**Orchallian Order, The**: an Order of Seers; Mother Alder is one of them.
**Order of the Arcane**: the wizard members of the Tower of the Arcane

## The Evermerians
**Ebert Cook:** (deceased)
**Duchess Morgovia of House Falstad**: ruler of Evermere
**Moby and Toby**: brothers; the "beloveds" of Penny. (deceased)
**Penny**: a tiny wisp of a girl (deceased)
**Rasker**: he guards the Duchess's warehouse (deceased)
**Rendon, Lord**: a noble of Evermere
**Slint**: aka the "scarecrow"; the Duchess's henchman (deceased)
**Trern**: he guards the Duchess's warehouse (deceased)

## People of The Hollow

**Azrael**: alchemist/tinker/wizard/Eternal
Bron Mason
**Constable, The**: chief lawman of The Hollow; the marshals report to him.
Ebert Cook: a cook

**Falstad, Lady Dahlia:** sister of Cassandra
Farthing, Duke Baltan, of Farthing Heights (deceased)
**Farthing, Lady (Duchess) Cassandra Falstad**
**Farthing, Miss Pennebray:** daughter of Lady Cassandra
**Marple Butler**: Azrael's butler / lead servant
**Mashals, The**: lawmen of The Hollow
**Mayor Barnton:** mayor of The Hollow
**Mikel Potter:** a skilled potter.
**Refisal**: Azrael's elderly gnome assistant
Rit Bowman
Triber Blacksmith
Widow Lothborg: enemy of Lady Cassandra Farthing

**People of Mindletown**
A town of several hundred folks within Eotrus demesne. The Odinhall is their most secure building. All listed are missing, dead, or presumed dead, except for Pellan.
**Alchemist, the**: town council member of Mindletown (deceased)
Baker, The and sons: townsfolk of Mindletown
**Butcher, the**: town council member of Mindletown
Cobbler: townsman of Mindletown; lives across the street from the alchemist
Constable Granger: constable of Mindletown
Farmer Smythe: a townsman of Mindletown (deceased)
Iceman: an ice merchant that sells his ice to Mindletown; hails from the northwest.
Innman: an innkeeper in Mindletown

Mikar Trapper: a trapper that sells his wares in Mindletown
Miller and his sons: townsmen of Mindletown
**Old Cern**: town elder of Mindletown (deceased)
Old Marvik: a Mindletown merchant that lived across from the alchemist
**Pellan**: the "beardless dwarf"; a town council member of Mindletown and former Captain in Dor Eotrus''s guard
Tanner, Mileson: a townsman of Mindletown
Thom Prichard: a townsman of Mindletown (deceased)
Wheelwright and his wife: townsfolk of Mindletown (both deceased)

## Others of Note

**Azathoth**: god worshipped by the Lords of Nifleheim and The Shadow League/The League of Light; his followers call him the "one true god".
**Azura du Marnian, the Seer**: Seer based in Tragoss Mor. Now travels with the Alders on *The Gray Talon*.
**Harbinger of Doom, The**: legendary, perhaps mythical, being that led a rebellion against Azathoth
**Jaros, the Blood Lord**: foe of Sir Gabriel Garn
**McDuff the Mighty**: a dwarf of many talents
**Pipkorn, Grandmaster**: (aka Rascatlan) former Grand Master of the Tower of the Arcane. A wizard.
**Shadow League, The** (aka The League of Shadows; aka The League of Light): alliance of individuals and groups collectively seeking to

bring about the return of Azathoth to Midgaard
**Valkyries**: sword maidens of the gods. They choose worthy heroes slain in battle and conduct them to Valhalla.

## Titles

**Archmage / Archwizard**: honorific title for a highly skilled wizard
**Archseer**: honorific title for a highly skilled seer
**Arkon**: a leader/general in service to certain gods and religious organizations
**Battle Mage**: a wizard whose skills are combat oriented.
**Castellan**: the commander of a fortress/Dor; in service to the Dor Lord.
**Constable:** chief law enforcement officer of a village or town.
**Dor Lord:** the leader of a fortress; usually a noble, and often the Patriarch/Matriach of a noble House.
**Freesword**: an independent soldier or mercenary
**Grandmaster**: honorific title for a senior wizard of the Tower of the Arcane.
**Hedge Wizard**: a wizard specializing in potions and herbalism, and/or minor magics.
**High Cleric**: the senior priest of a church/temple, or of a religious order.
**High Magister**: a member of Lomion's Tribunal.
**High Priest**: the senior priest of a church/temple, or of a religious order.
**House Cleric**: the senior priest in service to a noble House
**House Wizard**: a senior wizard in service to a

noble House
**Leren**: (pronounced Lee-rhen) generic title for a physician
**Mage**: a practioner of magic; a wizard.
**Magling**: a young or inexperienced wizard; also, a derogatory term for a wizard.
**Marshal**: a law enforcement officer; typically reports to a Constable of village or town.
**Master Oracle**: a highly skilled seer.
**Master Scout**: the chief scout/hunter/tracker of a fortress or noble House.
**Par**: honorific title for a wizard
**Seer** (sometimes, "Seeress"): women with supernatural powers to see past/present/future events.
**Sorcerer**: a practitioner of magic; a wizard.
**Tower Mage**: a wizard that his a member of the Order of the Arcane.
**Weapons Master**: the senior weapon's instructor/trainer/officer at a fortress.
**Wizard**: practitioners of magic

# THINGS

<u>Miscellany</u>
**Alder Stone, The**: a Seer Stone held by House Alder
**Asgardian Daggers**: legendary weapons created in the first age of Midgaard. They can harm creatures of Nifleheim.
**Bellowing Banshee, The:** one of the ships lost in the Fens
**Bloodlust, The**: name for the affliction affecting people in The Hollow

**Chapterhouse**: base/manor/fortress of a knightly order
**Dargus Dal**: Asgardian dagger, previously Gabriel's, now Theta's
**Dor:** a generic Lomerian word meaning "fortress"
**Dyvers Blades**: finely crafted steel swords
**Dyvers Thraysk**: a short wide sword.
**Ether, The:** invisible medium that exists everywhere and within which the weave of magic travels/exists.
**Granite Throne, The**: the name of the king's throne in Lomion City. To "sit the granite throne" means to be the king.
**Mages and Monsters**: a popular, tactical war game that uses miniatures
**Mithril**: precious metal of great strength and relative lightness
**Ragnarok**: prophesied battle between the Aesir and the Nifleites.
**Ranal**: a black metal, hard as steel and half as heavy, weapons made of it can affect creatures of chaos
**Seer Stones**: magical "crystal balls" that can see far-off events.
**Weave of Magic**; aka the Magical Weave: the source of magic
**Yggdrasill:** sacred tree that supports and/or connects the Nine Worlds

**Languages of Midgaard**
**Lomerian:** the common tongue of Lomion and much of the known world
**Magus Mysterious**: olden language of sorcery
**Militus Mysterious**: olden language of sorcery

used by certain orders of knights
**Old High Lomerian**: an olden dialect of Lomerian

## Military Units of Lomion
**Squad**: a unit of soldiers typically composed of 3 to 8 soldiers, but it can be as few as 2 or as many as 15 soldiers.
**Squadron:** a unit of soldiers typically composed of two to four squads, totaling about 30 soldiers, including officers.

## Military Ranks of Lomion
(from junior to senior)
Trooper; Corporal; Sergeant; Lieutenant (a knight is considered equivalent in rank to a Lieutenant); Captain; Knight Captain (for units with Knights); Commander; Knight Commander (for units with Knights); Lord Commander (if a noble); General (for Regiment sized units or larger)

## ABOUT GLENN G. THATER

For more than twenty-five years, Glenn G. Thater has written works of fiction and historical fiction that focus on the genres of epic fantasy and sword and sorcery. His published works of fiction include the first ten volumes of the *Harbinger of Doom* saga: *Gateway to Nifleheim*; *The Fallen Angle*; *Knight Eternal*; *Dwellers of the Deep*; *Blood, Fire, and Thorn*; *Gods of the Sword*; *The Shambling Dead*; *Master of the Dead*; *Shadow of Doom*; *Wizard's Toll*; the novella, *The Gateway*; and the novelette, *The Hero and the Fiend*.

Mr. Thater holds a Bachelor of Science degree in Physics with concentrations in Astronomy and Religious Studies, and a Master of Science degree in Civil Engineering, specializing in Structural Engineering. He has undertaken advanced graduate study in Classical Physics, Quantum Mechanics, Statistical Mechanics, and Astrophysics, and is a practicing licensed professional engineer specializing in the multidisciplinary alteration and remediation of buildings, and the forensic investigation of building failures and other disasters.

Mr. Thater has investigated failures and collapses of numerous structures around the United States and internationally. Since 1998, he has been a member of the American Society of Civil Engineers' Forensic Engineering Division (FED), is a Past Chairman of that Division's Executive Committee and FED's Committee on Practices to

Reduce Failures. Mr. Thater is a LEED (Leadership in Energy and Environmental Design) Accredited Professional and has testified as an expert witness in the field of structural engineering before the Supreme Court of the State of New York.

Mr. Thater is an author of numerous scientific papers, magazine articles, engineering textbook chapters, and countless engineering reports. He has lectured across the United States and internationally on such topics as the World Trade Center collapses, bridge collapses, and on the construction and analysis of the dome of the United States Capitol in Washington D.C.

**CONNECT WITH GLENN G. THATER ONLINE**

**Glenn G. Thater's Website:**
http://www.glenngthater.com

To be notified about new book releases and any special offers or discounts regarding Glenn's books, please join his mailing list here: http://eepurl.com/vwubH

**BOOKS BY GLENN G. THATER**

**THE HARBINGER OF DOOM SAGA**
**GATEWAY TO NIFLEHEIM**
**THE FALLEN ANGLE**
**KNIGHT ETERNAL**
**DWELLERS OF THE DEEP**
**BLOOD, FIRE, AND THORN**
**GODS OF THE SWORD**

**THE SHAMBLING DEAD**
**MASTER OF THE DEAD**
**SHADOW OF DOOM**
**WIZARD'S TOLL**
VOLUME 11+ *forthcoming*

**THE HERO AND THE FIEND**
(A novelette set in the Harbinger of Doom universe)

**THE GATEWAY**
(A novella length version of *Gateway to Nifleheim*)

**HARBINGER OF DOOM**
(Combines *Gateway to Nifleheim* and *The Fallen Angle* into a single volume)

**THE DEMON KING OF BERGHER**
(A short story set in the Harbinger of Doom universe)

Visit Glenn G. Thater's website at http://www.glenngthater.com for the most current list of my published books.